The Red Door

and Other Stories

K. E. Karl

Softback ISBN 979-8-9870141-3-4
eBook ISBN 979-8-9870141-4-1

LCCN 2023921311

An earlier version of "The Run to Lesotho" first appeared in *The Pennsylvania Literary Journal*. It was also Chapter 21 of *Our Man in Mbabane* by K. E. Karl, a novel based on the author's true-life experience in Southern Africa supporting the fight against apartheid in the late 1970s and early 1980s.

These stories originally appeared, in different form, in the following publications: "The Red Door" in *Evening Street Review*, "Webern's Lament" in *Lowestoft Chronicle*, and "The Stolen Bicycle" in *Gumshoe Review*.

Book design by Barış Şehri

For Arthur Erskine McClymonds

CONTENTS

WEBERN'S LAMENT

"What's that music?" Evan asked. "It sounds like it's from a horror film." Evan, my neighbor, had decided to drop by my southwest-facing condo so he could get a good view of the sunset. My expectation of a quiet dinner listening to some of my favorite music vanished.

"It's Anton Webern's Four Songs, Opus 13," I replied. "I'll turn it down." Few people like Webern's music. Rather than lowering the volume, I switched it off to enjoy later. Along with Schoenberg and Berg, Webern was a master of the twelve-tone technique. But much of it is atonal, making it difficult for fans of Bach, Beethoven, or The Beatles. I knew Evan liked jazz but doubted he ever listened to classical music.

"Can I get you a glass of wine?" I was mid-pour since I knew the answer.

"Need you ask? Thanks. I dropped by to watch the sunset with you. Your view is better than mine."

"I'm honored. I thought it was the wine."

"That too, of course!"

"Will you be staying for dinner this evening also?"

"What a delightful idea. Thank you for the invite. Turn Weber back on and tell me about him."

"It's *Webern*," I said, heavily emphasizing the *n*.

"Yes, just as I said."

"He was a pupil of Arnold Schoenberg, who taught him the twelve-tone technique. He composed thirty-one pieces in his lifetime, and they are short. His sole symphony takes only about nine minutes to play. We're listening to his Complete Works conducted by Boulez. They fit on three CDs. In contrast, it takes about 170 CDs for all of Mozart's music, and he didn't live long. The Nazis denounced Webern's music as 'degenerate art.' Ironically, at the end of World War II, Webern was shot dead by an American soldier in a tragic mistake. He was sixty-one years old."

"Boulez?"

"Pierre Boulez. A famous French composer and conductor."

"Of course. I knew that. Shame about Weber's untimely death."

"Your wine, Evan," I said, handing him a glass of Gavi and biting back another correction of his mispronunciation of Webern.

"Thanks. And what's for dinner?"

"I'm not sure. I'll have to thaw something from the freezer. Shrimp, scallops, mussels?"

"Scallops, thanks. That would be lovely."

"As you wish. I'll cook it in wine and butter and sprinkle chives on it. We'll have it over linguine."

"Sounds delightfully delicious!"

"We'll see," I said.

Evan was medium height, portly, with flush-red cheeks and thinning hair. Though old enough to retire, he had recently taken up a position at a software company that analyzed collateralized loan obligations, or CLOs. Evan knew the CLO market and, importantly, many CLO buyers. On the other hand, the kids he worked with were experts in programming data analytic tools. A match made in financial heaven. In his spare time, he indulged in his favorite pastimes: eating and drinking. He also liked long walks and visiting museums. Accompanying him to a museum often presented a social dilemma due to his unfortunate condition of excess flatulence. One could not view paintings alongside him, lest the other viewers surmise you to be the culprit. Nevertheless, he was always jovial company.

"Marvelous sunset, simply spectacular."

"I'm glad you're enjoying it. Another glass of wine?"

"Don't mind if I do. Don't get up; I'll fetch it myself." Evan rose from his chair, facing the window, and bounded across the room with surprising alacrity for someone of sixty-five years who had just knocked back a glass of wine like it was soda pop. He poured himself a generous splash and returned to his seat to gaze out of the floor-to-ceiling windows, which offered a mostly unobstructed view of the horizon. My condo also has a balcony, but it was an early November evening, too chilly to watch the sky from outside.

"You're a good friend, Frank."

"Thank you."

"I'm sure you're astonished to hear that I thoroughly enjoy this music."

"I'm flabbergasted but also flattered."

Just then a knock on the door rolled across the condo. I went to the entry and found Audrey waiting to return the screwdriver I had lent her.

"Who is it?" Evan shouted from the other room.

"It's Audrey," I shouted back.

"Audrey, come on in! We're having wine and watching the sunset. Frank's invited us to dinner—scallops."

"Oh, thank you, Frank. That's very kind," Audrey said as she handed me the tool and brushed past me. "Don't mind me. I can pour the wine myself. What do we have? Oh, a Gavi. Excellent."

"Sure. Help yourself," I said. *What is my place—a restaurant?*

A phone rang, and Evan and Audrey simultaneously reached for their cell phones. It was Audrey's, and she answered it while walking toward the windows—glass in one hand, phone in the other—to view the changing sky as she listened.

"Great," she said. "Well, why don't you join us? We're all having dinner at Frank's. Fabulous. See you soon."

"Frank, that was Geraldine. She'd love to have dinner and thanked you profusely for the invitation."

"I'm charmed," I said. *Chez Frank: no reservations required!*

The sunset began as a yellow band across the horizon, interrupted only by two monolithic buildings. As the night progressed, its color shifted to orange, then red, the sky above bleeding from light into midnight blue. Inky clouds slashed the skyline, creating cutouts in the orange backdrop. The nearby towers were black against the crimson sky, except for the dots of white light emanating from a few windows. The two monoliths would soon display a colorful light show, but not before darkness engulfed the panorama.

"How's dinner coming, Frank?" Evan asked. "I'm famished."

"I'm still thawing the scallops." *Or perhaps, Le Bistrot Frank, avec un service attentionné.*

"Frank, what is this ghastly music?" Audrey said. "You're not playing Schoenberg, are you?"

"It's Webern, not Schoenberg," I replied.

"Even more appalling," Audrey said.

"Evan quite likes it."

"Yes, it's stupendous," Evan said. "Marvelously chaotic. I love it."

"Oh, you two. Incorrigible. But I suppose I can live with it."

"Thanks," I said. "That's big of you." *I'm glad they're not going to fight about the music. The evening has only just begun.*

Audrey, tall and slim, with elegantly coiffed gray hair, settled herself into one of my "Star-Trek" chairs. Made of Koa wood from Hawaii, they have a seat that curves around your buttocks and a high, thin back. Instead of four legs, there is just one large, elegantly sculpted leg with two long feet poking forward. Audrey had retired years ago from a consulting job at one of the Big Four accounting firms and recently settled herself in my building in a north-facing unit. When not reading books about art and classical music, she busied herself socializing, visiting museums, and attending concerts.

"Oh, that's my friend Alfred," Evan said, responding to the tune on his phone. "Hello, Alfred. You're nearby? We're having dinner at Frank's this evening. Hurry up so you can catch the end of the sunset. Yes, see you soon." Evan disconnected the call and casually said, "That was Alfred. He'll be joining us for dinner."

"Yes, I heard," I said. *It should be a good crowd. They have a lot in common; everyone loves to bicker.*

"Thank you," Evan said. "It's so generous of you to have us on such short notice, Frank."

"Yes," I said. *Am I enjoying myself? Or just playacting as the host? I like these people, but perhaps I would have preferred a quiet evening?*

I unlocked the front door, so the other guests could let themselves in, opened another bottle of wine, set out two more glasses, took more scallops out to thaw, and began preparing dinner.

Geraldine and Alfred arrived, poured themselves a glass of wine, and joined Audrey and Evan, viewing the sunset.

"Do we want anchovies with our romaine lettuce salad?" I asked. A chorus of *Nos* settled the matter. However, a similar request about parmesan cheese was answered in the affirmative.

"Frank, this wine isn't chilled sufficiently," Alfred said. Alfred had been a surgeon and only recently left his practice. Over the years, he had become so accustomed to commanding precision in the operating theater that he expected it in his private life from everyone as well. I nodded and put the bottle in the freezer, mollifying him. We were all used to his prickliness and paid it no mind. Short, rail-thin with a shaved head, it was impossible to take his brusqueness seriously; it was just the way he was.

Having made the salad, I turned my attention to the scallops. It's a simple dish. First, sauté the scallops in olive oil, taking care not to overcook them, then remove them from the pan. Next, add butter, salt, pepper, and finely diced shallots to the pan, and cook them until soft. Finally, pour in a glass of white wine, some water from the boiled pasta, reintroduce the scallops to the mix, chuck in some chopped chives, the cooked linguine, stir, and voilà!

"What are you making, Frank?" Geraldine asked.

"Scallops linguine," I replied.

"It smells divine," she said.

"Thank you. Let's hope it tastes that way."

"I'm sure it will," Geraldine said. "It's very kind of you to invite us to dinner and share your view." Geraldine was short, plump, and with hair dyed a shocking shade of scarlet. It had an effect. Something like waving a red flag at a bull.

"Yes, and fortunately, I had sufficient scallops for the five of us," I said.

"But what is this music?" Geraldine asked.

"Webern. His complete works. It should just take us through the evening. I know you're excited."

"Yes. Of course. I'll just turn it down if you don't mind."

"Evan might object."

"We'll see about that," Geraldine said.

"Don't touch that dial!" Evan said, beginning the customary Geraldine-Evan spat, though sooner in the evening than usual. Generally, it started after both had drunk two glasses of wine, but tonight we would be treated to an early rendition of an all-too-familiar act.

"I can't hear it," Evan said as Alfred stepped in between the two of them, who had squared off, their hands on their hips, glaring intently at each other.

"Why don't we lower the volume only a bit as a compromise," Alfred suggested to Geraldine. "Then, Evan can hear it, but it will be less oppressive for you."

"Fine. That's fair," Geraldine said, adjusting the volume to suit both of them.

"Louder!" Evan said.

"OK, but only a little," Geraldine responded. "And that's loud enough."

"I think I can live with it," Evan said.

"Good!" Geraldine said, prompting a low growl from Evan.

"More wine, anyone?" I asked, pulling the bottle from the freezer and placing another two inside. I thought a bottle each might just get us through the evening.

"I don't mind if I do," Alfred said, failing to notice the temperature had barely budged.

While I prepared dinner, my four guests became deeply involved in a conversation about the Jaspar Johns exhibit at the Philadelphia Museum of Art. Only Evan had seen the other half of the show at the Whitney, so he attempted to regale them with how much better it was than the Philly one but only irritated everyone. While Alfred and Evan preferred the Johns show, Audrey and Geraldine argued vociferously for the superiority of Emma Amos's works, also on view at the museum. According to the two women, she was only less famous than Johns because she was Black and female. I observed the histrionics, complete with wild gesticulations, from the safety of the kitchen area, Webern's music bolstering the tumultuousness of the debate.

"All those flags, numbers, and hatch mark paintings are tedious and repetitive," Audrey said. "Whereas Amos's work is highly creative and affirmative of women and African Americans. What's Jaspar's work affirmative of? Himself! Nothing more."

"I disagree," Alfred said. "Johns's work is quintessentially affirmative of America, which is a good thing, given all the lousy press we get overseas."

"You need to see the whole exhibit to fully appreciate Johns's contribution to art," Evan said.

"You split the infinitive, Evan," Audrey said.

"Oh, *please,*" Evan responded.

"Yes, enough, Evan," Geraldine said. "I'm sure the Whitney exhibit is much the same as the Philadelphia show. Amos's work is uplifting, and the Johns's stuff is mostly depressing. There is just no comparison."

"Dinner is ready," I interjected. *I wish their discussion could be more cordial, more copacetic. But isn't this who they are and what they enjoy?*

I had set the table for five with myself at the head, well-placed to intervene in case of any further altercations. Everyone grabbed a seat with the ladies on my right, facing the windows, and the men on my left, viewing the room. Too late, I realized Geraldine was across from Evan, and Alfred was facing Audrey.

"So, why haven't you retired yet, Evan?" Geraldine demanded as she dove into her plate of pasta, applying her unique vacuum-cleaner eating technique.

"I'm quite enjoying my work, and the young people I work with keep me youthful," Evan replied.

"What nonsense," Geraldine said. "It's unseemly for someone of your age to be still working so many hours."

"I enjoy it greatly; it hardly seems like work at all," Evan said. "Just because you like retirement doesn't mean it is for everyone."

"Life is meant to be lived in a cycle," Geraldine said. "We're born, we attend school, we work, we marry and have children, and then we retire. It's as simple as that!"

"But you never married, nor did you have kids," Alfred said.

"Quite so!" Evan said.

"That's beside the point," Geraldine said. "The point is that there is a time and a place for everything, and it is your time to retire, Evan."

"I appreciate your interest in my life, but I'm happy to live it as I please," Evan said.

"I have been enjoying my work at the hospice," Alfred said, attempting to steer the conversation in another direction. "I find it gratifying helping people in their dying days. They appreciate a laugh, and a little kindness goes a long way."

"I can't think of anything more dreadful than attending to the terminally ill," Audrey said.

"You should try it; you might enjoy it," Alfred said. "Or perhaps you could help disadvantaged kids learn to read. There are plenty of worthwhile activities you can do to support our local community."

"I never seem to have the time to do everything I'd like," Audrey responded. "I have no idea where I would find the time to help children. Nor do I think I would be good at teaching them anything, let alone how to read."

"I get much more back than I put in," Alfred said. "It's gratifying to be engaging with people in a simple way, so much more pleasant than slicing people up while they lie immobile in front of you."

"Well, I should certainly hope so," I said.

"I give blood," Evan said.

"You've got a lot to give," Geraldine said.

"If you're referring to my weight..." Evan said.

"That's very socially responsible of you," Alfred interrupted. "Hospitals always need blood. How often do you give?"

"Once a year," Evan said. "I find it exhausting losing all that blood."

"Every pint helps," Alfred said.

"I tried providing my management skills to small businesses, but no one seemed interested in my help and advice," Geraldine said.

"That's hardly surprising," Evan said.

"I'll have you know that I was a very efficient manager of my clothing boutique," Geraldine responded.

And so, the conversation proceeded with the two general discussions I had heard many times before. First, is it better to continue working as long as you like, or should one retire and enjoy life? Second, should one devote time to the needy in one's waning years or simply enjoy a well-deserved respite after a long work life? Personally, I think each person should decide for themselves, but many people feel the need to persuade others toward their viewpoint.

"What's for dessert? I see you have pears," Audrey said, hinting that she would like my specialty—pears poached in white wine with lime zest, cinnamon, and a dash of Cointreau.

Another easy dish, and the table quieted mercifully as I served it.

"What's that music?" Audrey asked. "It changed abruptly."

"That's an arrangement by Webern of one of Bach's pieces," I said. "It will be followed by some songs by Schubert, also arranged by Webern."

"Oh, turn it up, please," Geraldine commanded, and I obliged.

"Now that's luscious and pleasant," Audrey said. Alfred and Evan looked at each other and nodded in agreement; it was calming.

"I liked Weber's pieces better," Evan said, causing Geraldine to direct a menacing scowl at him. "But this is good, too." Geraldine smiled, tilting her head back in appreciation.

The sun had long ago set, and city lights sparkled below us. I realized that this is how life should be: dinner with wine and good friends. The chaotic squabbling was simply the hum of human interaction, like the murmur of pigeons fighting over a scrap of bread or the babbling of water breaking over the rocks of a fast-running creek, the sun sparkling off the splashing drops. The music had changed the mood, relaxing old tensions, easing frayed nerves. Webern had delivered an evening of strife, then reconciliation. What more could you ask from a composer?

"Have more wine," I said, circling the table to ensure everyone had something in their glasses. "I'd like to propose a toast: To friends! May we always cherish each other."

THE RED DOOR

"You can't go in there," the uniformed man said as I yanked at the door handle.

"But we were in there at the bar just last week," I replied.

"There's no bar here," he responded. "There's never been a drinking establishment at this address."

"I don't understand..." I said.

"Frank, come away," Jane said. "It's OK. We'll get a drink somewhere else."

"But this is the place we always go for a drink after the movies."

"It must be somewhere else."

The doorman tilted his head and examined us quizzically but said nothing. We retreated out onto the sidewalk through the revolving glass doors, which I thought was the entrance to our favorite post-film watering hole.

It was a cool, agreeable Philadelphia afternoon in October; a slight breeze rustled through the tree leaves. We had just left the cinema. The "blockbuster" Bond movie had drawn a whopping ten percent capacity at the movie theater. No one was munching popcorn, and everyone was wearing a mask. As a retired economist, I wondered how these film venues would stay in business post-Covid.

"What happened?" I asked.

"We obviously have forgotten the address," Jane said.

"That's so odd. I was sure this was the entry. Oh, well, let's head toward home and see if we find another place. That's a shame, though; their Sauvignon Blanc was delightful."

"There'll be good wines at other bars," Jane said.

We walked down Walnut Street, heading west toward Rittenhouse Square, but didn't find anything suitable. Before reaching home, we took a shortcut through a less-familiar alley and walked past a red door.

"Wait a second," I said. "I hear something like talking and clinking of glasses. Do you know this place?"

"No. I've never noticed it before."

I walked up to the door and examined it. The only marking on it was two letters, "*e. e.*," burned into the shiny gloss of the crimson-painted entrance. I tried the handle, and it opened into a vestibule where a large man in a tailored suit was guarding another scarlet door with multiple panes of frosted glass.

"What's the password?" he asked.

"In just spring," I replied.

"Enter," he said, pushing the door open wide for us.

"This place is creepy," Jane said. "It's smoky too, but that isn't the smell of cigarettes. Are you sure you want to have a drink here?"

We looked around. The room was not large but a comfortable size for the twenty-or-so people we saw mingling inside. No one was wearing a mask, so we removed ours as we warily edged up to a couple of stools at the bar. It was a U-shape and had an island at its center with liquor bottles ascending it in a rich display of colors and shapes. The wine glasses dripping from the ceiling were partially obscured by the blue-gray haze that clung to the roof like a cloud on a smoggy day. The flip-up exit from the counter was to our left. A couple sat silently near it, their faces pinched from a recent argument.

"Sure. Why not? It's probably cash-only, but I have plenty."

"Suit yourself; you always do. How'd you know the password?"

"I assumed the place was associated with e. e. cummings, given the sign on the front entry. So, I gave the beginning line of one of his more famous poems."

"Clever boy. But that really dates us," Jane said.

"Well, we aren't young," I replied. "I even apparently misplace entire drinking places from time to time."

We took seats at the dark wooden counter and scanned the crowd. Most of the people were sitting at tables in the room surrounding the bar. It was a mixed group of people by age—a few young people, some middle-aged, a couple of older people.

"What'll it be?" the bartender asked.

"Two Deaths in the Afternoon," I replied.

"What did you order?" Jane asked after the barkeep turned away to mix the drinks.

"It's the only literary drink I know—Hemingway. It has absinthe and champagne in it. Plus, some syrup, I think."

"Absinthe?" Jane said, alarmed.

"It's perfectly safe and tastes like licorice," I said.

"I *detest* anise drinks," Jane said.

"Oh, good. Something different for you. If you don't like it, order something else, and I'll drink yours."

"So generous of you."

"Absolutely."

The drinks came, and Jane gingerly tasted the concoction, pronouncing it "not bad" and expressed admiration for the color and the flat, wide coupe glass.

While gazing at the other patrons, I noticed something strange.

"Jane, who does that guy over to our right look like to you?"

"Allen Ginsberg?"

"And sitting next to him?"

"What was his partner's name?"

I looked up *"Ginsberg's partner"* on my phone and said, "Peter Orlovsky." Eerily, one of the photos on my cell matched the couple at the table. They were both bearded and even had on similar clothes to the photo. Allen had on a sports coat and white shirt, a black overcoat at his side. Peter was wearing a red sports-team jacket over his gray shirt.

"It must be Beat Poet night here at the e. e. Red Door," I said. "No wonder there is a heavy smell of MJ in the air."

"A typical Philly scent, though usually outdoors," Jane said. "Say, isn't absinthe supposed to give you hallucinations?"

"Naw. That's an old myth propagated by prohibitionists. Supposedly a drug in wormwood was the problem. But today, if they make absinthe with wormwood, they take that drug out, but only for our reassurance; it never did have much of an impact."

"We could go over the top," Jane said. "I have medicinal candy if you like."

"You carry it with you?" I asked, shaking my head.

"I forgot to unload my purse."

"Marijuana usually gives me a depressing hangover," I said.

"This won't. It's a special high."

"OK. What the hell. Absinthe, MJ, and a time warp. What do I have to lose?"

Jane handed me a couple of green gummies, and I had to ask, "These gummi bears give you a high?"

"Yes, and they are tasty too," Jane replied.

We chewed the candies and reviewed our surroundings. With a modest passing of time and a few more sips of our cocktails, the decanters behind the bar became shinier and more colorful. The bottle of absinthe oscillated in color between dark green and chartreuse, while the whiskey's fluctuated from blackish brown to ruby red.

My hankering for a snack became palpable, so I asked the bartender for something to munch on, and he generously provided bowls of mixed spicy crunchies and peanuts. Jane and I could hardly contain ourselves, and the nibbles quickly disappeared.

"What about the others here?" Jane asked. "Any other writers?"

I searched on my phone for images of the Beat Generation while looking around the room.

"OK. Ferlinghetti is in the far corner. The guy nodding off in the back area is Burroughs, and the bartender is Kerouac.

"The bartender is Kerouac?" Jane said. Turning toward the man polishing glasses behind the bar, she said, "I loved *On the Road*."

"I'm glad, thanks," Jack said. "You should try *Big Sur*; that's my latest work. The protagonist, like me, is struggling with alcoholism. That's why I'm bartending; it's a therapy. I need to cut back on my drinking, but it's a huge temptation standing behind this counter."

"I hope it works," Jane replied. "You're so well regarded as an author. I'll get a copy of *Big Sur*."

"Thanks. But sometimes I think I might be too famous for my own good," Jack replied. "Enjoy your evening."

"He was nice," I whispered. "Tragically, he only lived to be forty-seven. We must look like old farts to him."

"I hate this ageism," Jane said. "Remember last week when we were at the Italian restaurant, and the young waitress was so insulting and unpleasant."

"We don't know it was ageism. Maybe that is her natural personality: rude and obnoxious."

"She was nice to the young people at the table next to ours. Friendly even."

"Whatever. We're not going to change it. I can see the headline: 'Old Farts Protest Ageism: Senior Citizens Occupy All the Benches in Rittenhouse Square.' People would jeer at us. Remember: we're in *Philly*."

"I suppose," Jane said, her face sagging at the thought of a demonstration.

"Maybe Allen will be friendly also," I suggested, emboldened by the weed and cocktail.

"We could try," Jane said uncertainly.

We approached their table, glasses in hand, and they both looked up at us expectantly.

"Excuse us, but you look like Allen Ginsberg," I said.

"I am," Allen said. "And this is Peter Orlovsky."

"I'm Frank, and this is Jane. Do you mind if we join you?" Allen waved a magnanimous hand, inviting us to sit.

"This is a most interesting bar," I said.

"It's our first time here," Jane added.

"We love it here and come all the time," Peter said. "Sometimes people give spontaneous poetry readings. Lawrence read one of his recent poems last night."

"And last week, Burroughs read an excerpt from his latest lyrical novel, *Nova Express*," Allen added. "Do either of you write?"

"I dabble a bit but have never been published," I said.

"Don't give up," Peter said. "You can only improve."

"I read," Jane said.

"That's important, especially if you buy books," Allen said.

"I do," Jane said, "and I just committed to buying a copy of *Big Sur*."

"Jack's in good form this evening," Peter said.

"We noticed. But he has chosen a very challenging therapy for his drinking problem," I said.

"True," Peter said. "He's holding up well under the circumstances."

"I'm inspired to read one of my poems now," Allen said, reaching into his coat and pulling out a single sheet of paper. Peter clinked his glass with a spoon, and the room immediately hushed in anticipation. It was a brief poem, more of a sing-song rant, against capitalists and our materialistic society, typical Ginsberg, but Jane and I listened with our mouths open in astonishment.

After the reading, Peter asked if we'd met Burroughs, who was sitting alone with his head slumped forward.

"I think he might like company," Peter said. So, Jane and I walked over to sit with William S.

"That was a deft way to get rid of us," Jane said as we crossed the room.

"Maybe they wanted time alone together. In any case, it was a pleasant pass-off."

We sat at Burroughs table, and he sluggishly lifted his head and asked, "Are you from Philadelphia?" After we replied in the affirmative, he asked if we knew where he could buy some horse.

"Horse meat?" Jane asked, aghast.

"He means heroin, Jane," I said.

"Unfortunately, neither of us use that drug, so we wouldn't know where to find any," Jane said. "We don't eat horse meat, either."

"Pity."

"I'm afraid I've only read *Naked Lunch*," I said. "Tell us about your latest novel."

"It's a Cosmic Consciousness Love Flesh Dream," he replied. "Exposing ersatz Immortality sewage of the Garden of Delight with so-called pornographic sections."

"Sounds delightful," Jane said, her eyes widening, more in horror than astonishment.

"It's challenging, but it's meant to be that way. We should all be experimenting with life and understanding the impact of the corporate-political world on our lives," Burroughs said. "When did they ever not take everything?"

"Yes, we have many issues in this country," Jane said. "I fear it is getting worse also. You were ahead of your time in your writing and your vision."

"That's generous. Unfortunately, I need to get back to my apartment. I wish you both a lovely evening."

"Thank you. We'd like to listen to Ferlinghetti before we go," I said. "Thanks for your time."

"Anytime. No time. Only minutes to go," Burroughs said with a wry smile.

"It was a pleasure meeting you," Jane said as we rose from our chairs and Burroughs headed for the front door.

"He's kind of scary, don't you think?" Jane asked.

"Prescient," I replied.

Ferlinghetti was in the corner, surrounded by young fans. Unfortunately, there were no available chairs, so Jane and I stood, joining the small admiration society in nodding our heads as Lawrence spoke.

Momentarily, he lifted his head and said, "Welcome, friends. Who might you be?"

We introduced ourselves, and a couple of generous students offered their chairs, embarrassing us, but we thanked them and sat down as it would have been impolite to do otherwise.

"Such a contrast to that waitress last week," Jane whispered in my ear, and I dipped my head quickly in agreement.

"We were discussing Ezra Pound, who, as you know, came into disrepute after he publicly supported the Italian Fascists in World War II," Lawrence said. "However misguided that was, I believe his literary work, particularly *The Cantos,* was extraordinary and is essential reading for aspiring poets."

"It's not an easy work," I said.

"No. But it's an epic and has many allusions to Greek myths and the like," Lawrence said. "Pound was a master of allusion, and this is what makes *The Cantos* a great work of poetry. Of course, you may also want to read my latest work, *Routines*. It's thirteen short improvisable plays about understanding Existence. Experimental madness."

"OK. I'll give them a try," I said.

"Good," Lawrence said. "Read, write, publish. That's my advice to all of you, and now I will bid you goodnight."

We all stood, and he shook hands with each of us before disappearing through a red curtain labeled *"Employees Only"* at the back of the bar.

The students headed to the bar for another round, leaving us sitting with our drinks at two push-together tables.

"Do you get the feeling we are getting shuttled along by the writers?" Jane asked.

"Everyone is busy," I said. "And they were all cordial."

"I'm dizzy," Jane said abruptly.

"OK. I'm not sure I could make it through another round either. But it has been fascinating. It reminds me of the time I was at the City Tavern and chatted with Ben Franklin."

I paid for our drinks at the bar, and we wobbled home, the sun glaring at us for the duration of our journey.

The following week, after another film at the same theatre, we found our favorite post-movie bar on Chestnut Street, where it had always been.

"I must have gotten the address wrong last week," I said. "Though I was sure we were at the right building."

"Never mind," Jane said. "We found it this time."

After we finished our glasses of white wine, Jane suggested we drop by the Red Door on the way home. We found the entrance. The paint had faded to a dark pink and was peeling. Where the *"e. e."* had been, there was a deep, violent gash in the wood.

I pounded heavily on the door, but there was no response.

MEMORIES OF A MISSPENT YOUTH

It was the summer of '74, and I had a week before my gig started with the Oregon State Highway Department, so I decided to visit my granddad in Hemet, California. I had just graduated from the University of Oregon, so felt I deserved a vacation. I'd take a bus down and get a ride home with my mom and sister, who were also planning on visiting him but a little later than me. Mom's dad was old, and this would likely be the last time I saw him. He'd always been kind to me, indulgent even. I suppose I was secretly hoping to connect with him emotionally, since there was so little of that in my immediate family. Dream on, dude.

Why did I want to visit my granddad, you might ask? Having grown up in a totally dysfunctional family, I was still, naively, searching for a connection with my relatives. It never occurred to me to think: what family life did Mom have when she grew up? What about Dad? Could that be why our family life was so crazy?

Mom was the oldest and took the brunt of all the rigid family-rearing techniques popular during her generation.

After the first child, the parenting efforts petered out, so the younger ones had it easier. My mom was a tough cookie and weathered it well, I'm sure, making it easier for her sister and brother. What we understood from occasional tales from Mom was that her dad was very restrictive and reserved. She wanted to go to New York for college, so she was excited when she heard she would study in Manhattan.

Kansas State University, in Manhattan, Kansas. Not exactly where she'd hoped.

She started taking pilot license exams, but Granddad put his foot down and prevented her from continuing. It wasn't ladylike. Granddad had a view about the status of his family (he was listed in *Who's Who in America*) and believed in keeping up appearances.

Grandma apparently wasn't warm and fuzzy, either. She had lost a couple of kids in miscarriages and was often depressed. So, not surprisingly, our mom was cool and aloof. She raised us, her kids, in the same way she was brought up, except for some softening via Dr. Spock's famous book. She was a flamboyant character, so that was fun, but that did not translate into paying much attention to us kids. Mom loved us but did not know how to express it. She read a book at some point that said you should hug those you love and rub their back. This resulted in bear hugs from Mom, with painful strokes along the spine. Mom did not do affection.

On my dad's side, the relatives were easy; there weren't any. At least, not that we knew of, except his mom. His dad died before he reached one and his mom was prone to mental breakdowns. I have fond memories of that grandmother, but of the three of us kids, I'm the only one. Apparently, on the second of her two visits to our family in Oregon, she had an emotional collapse. I was too young to understand or remember, but my older siblings did. We never visited her in Kansas, so we never met Dad's uncles, aunts, and cousins, of which there were many. I only heard about them after Dad died and one of his cousins phoned me to offer his condolences and invited me to visit his B&B, so we could meet.

OK. So, you're a kid growing up on a farm in Kansas with an erratic mother as your immediate family. What do you do when you graduate from college? Exactly! You get as far away as possible. For Mom and Dad, that was Oregon. This was in 1947 or so—Hawaii and Alaska weren't states then and Maine was cold. Why not California, you ask? Easy: Granddad was there, and my dad and he did not get along; Mom had married beneath her social status, according to Gramps.

Do you think Dad could have resented Granddad's view of him? Here's a story. Granddad would send me silver dollars he collected from banks at one-dollar bill each. He'd ask the teller if they had any, and when they did, he swapped a paper bill for one. Then he'd send them to me because he knew I collected coins. I eventually got up to twenty silver dollars. But I wanted a bike. So, my dad said, "I'll make you a deal. You put in twenty dollars, and I'll put in twenty dollars, and we'll get you a bike. Deal?" I fell for it; I figured Granddad's access to silver coins was limitless. But, of course, that was the last year he sent me one. Yep. Those two had a swell relationship.

That was the family lives of my parents, so you can imagine our family of five—parents, my brother, my sister, and me—were a loving, caring, supporting bunch. Right? More like insane nuclear warfare every night. But I couldn't see that—it was normal to me, so it didn't occur to me it might be difficult to connect with my distant relatives.

What was it like? Mom and Dad would knock back a couple of martinis each night before dinner and place a third on the table to sip while eating. Then they would have at each other. The fusillades of caustic remarks would light up the dinner sky, flying between Dad and Mom like in one of those war movies with flares, rockets, and tracer bullets. Randomly, one of us would get into the line of fire with verbal assaults or a spoon rap on the head. Do you think their fighting had anything to do with Dad's extramarital affairs? Nah. When they finally divorced—about a decade after this summer—he had four girlfriends. How do you manage four liaisons in a small town? I can't imagine anyone could go undetected with one affair, let alone four. Finally, one of Mom's friends blurted out that she had seen Dad with his girlfriend Kate at a bar the other evening. This "friend" had assumed Mom and Dad had a European understanding and Mom knew all about Dad's mistresses. Mom *did* know but couldn't admit it to herself; there was no understanding, just denial. Now, she couldn't ignore it. Embarrassed, she filed for divorce.

I was the youngest, so mostly passed under the radar. School was easy for me, and I didn't have any emotional issues that I was aware of (or admitted to), so I did pretty much whatever I wanted. I'd just tell my parents, "I'm hitchhiking to Pennsylvania to see my girlfriend." (I cover that below.) And off I went. None of this "that's too dangerous, you can't do that" from them. It was benign neglect. Not an uncommon parenting strategy in the '50s to early '70s. Or, "I'm getting an apartment with my girlfriend this year in Portland." Big hullaballoo, but they couldn't say "No!" They had never told me what to do. Or helped. When it came to college, I applied to one school, Reed College, and got wait-listed. I had no backup. But I got in. After two years, Dad told me my tuition funds were exhausted. Why he waited two years to tell me this, I have no clue. It came out of the blue. So, I quit college, but working sucked (state highway department, my first year was in Pendleton, Oregon—a great town, but total boondocks after Portland). So, I applied to the University of Oregon and got automatically accepted a week before classes started in the fall of '72. I made just enough money that summer to pay my tuition and rent; food stamps took care of the rest. The people who handed out the stamps at the government office treated me like a freeloading douchebag; a small price to pay—I couldn't have survived without them.

The summer after high school, I couldn't get my job back at Taco Time—my hair was too long. Small town. So, I hitched to the East Coast to stay with my girlfriend, Val, in Kennett Square. Yep. Same one. It was an on-again, off-again relationship for five years. Long story. Some other time.

Things were going fine in Pennsylvania. I would relax in her sister's apartment where she also stayed, go for walks, bike rides, and read a lot. It was a pleasant pre-college break. When there were thunderstorms, the three of us would dance in the rain in the nearby cornfields. They both worked at a restaurant/ice cream parlor. I chilled.

Then, Val booted me out.

Apparently, my slothful attitude toward life jarred with her working ethics. Or maybe her sister was sick of me.

Who knows? With nowhere to stay, I stuck out my thumb and explored the Northeast. My Uncle Bob, who lived on Long Island, wasn't far away, so I headed north. I had fond memories of him because he played chess with me when I was young; no one else would (I was too good at it). I was camping out, hitching, and had some cash saved up from working at Taco Time when my hair was shorter, i.e. before my senior year. I made it into New York City, and it was great—I legally bought a six-pack of beer! Michelob. Might as well get the best. But, where to drink it? I found a park, but people glared at me. Unperturbed, I headed for Long Island figuring I could stay with my uncle and travel into the city to see the sites—visit museums, Statue of Liberty, Coney Island, whatever. That didn't work out so well.

On the second day I was visiting my Uncle Bob and his wife, Kitty, they took me to a barbecue with some of their friends, one of whom asked me, "So, how long are you staying with your aunt and uncle?" Before I could answer, Kitty interjected, "Oh, he's leaving tomorrow for New York City." She said this as if referring to a foreign country—it couldn't be a day trip. Do you think I felt welcome to stay longer? This wasn't even a hint; it was a command. So, the next day I bid adieu to them and headed for Maine where you could camp out. I had a stop in Provincetown, another disastrous interlude. More on that later.

I had excellent digs for my last two years in college: fifty dollars a month for a room with a kitchen alcove and a bathroom down the hall. For my first year in the studio, there were no other tenants, so I had the bathroom to myself. It was the next best thing to having the toilet and bathtub in my apartment.

But then my landlord disappeared.

He was a real estate agent, and his offices were below my place—I had the whole second floor of a mixed-use, commercial, and residential house on High Street in Eugene. My too-small-for-me, green-framed, ten-speed bike took me everywhere local, my thumb everywhere distant.

Anyway, one night my landlord vanished. They found his eyeglasses stained with his blood on his abandoned Mercedes near a quarry outside of town. They never found him. I was so glad I had slept over at a friend's place. I had a rock-solid alibi. People speculated it was the mafia, but the Cosa Nostra in Bluejeans, Oregon? A hippie cult thing would have been more likely (making me a suspect!), but why a boring business guy? Really, my secret theory was that he just wanted to get away from it all and was in the Caribbean sipping piña coladas and enjoying the local scenery if you get my drift. His wife was a paraplegic, and maybe he had become tired of his girlfriend. Who knows? He was gone. He was the best landlord I ever had; I'd pay the rent, and he'd ignore me. You could do anything at night. Smoking dope. No problem. Wild parties. No problem. He wasn't there!

But then, he really *wasn't* there, and his kids sold the business to some young whizzes who wanted to leverage their new asset. They quickly rented the two rooms across the hall, and I had to share the bathroom. Outrageous! The only good news was that they didn't start charging me extra rent; it stayed at fifty bucks.

The new tenants were all very interesting. A real trip. And they were yin and yang, good and bad, or maybe even good and ugly. My family for my last year in college.

On the positive side, we had four refugees from a commune in southern Oregon: Drizza Goldberg, the Amazing Rozetta, Big Red Thornton, and the infamous Black Robert. Drizza was tall, blond, and perfectly shaped for her job as a topless waitress in a sleazy bar. And, yes, waitress, that's what they were called in '74. Server, smerver. Get a life.

The Amazing Rozetta was an exotic dancer at a different but equally sordid bar. These refugees-from-a-commune had chosen these jobs for one reason: the money. They were the highest paying gigs they could get, and they wanted to save some dough before returning to their home, since jobs were scarce near their commune. I visited it one weekend; it was in the middle of fucking nowhere.

Rozetta came to show me her handmade costumes one day. They were small but a bit bigger than a G-string. I had no idea that topless dancers made their own costumes. She laid them out carefully on the floor of my pad and asked me which was my favorite. They were all see-through with sequins, feathers, and patches of shiny fabric. Feathers seemed a natural choice, so I picked that one. What was I to do? Was she trying to hit on me? What could she possibly see in me? She offered me some cocaine, and I tasted it; it numbed my mouth, concluding my only lifetime experience with coke.

Then, I had to go.

I was deep into politics those days and had volunteered to distribute leaflets promoting the United Farm Workers in front of a store selling scab produce. We were boycotting grapes, as I recall. The customers loved us; little old ladies would poke us with their umbrellas when they passed us to enter the supermarket.

Anyway, after I split abruptly, Rozetta understood I wasn't into her, and I never had to review costumes again. However, Val, my girlfriend, and I went to see her perform—at Rozetta's request. Our job was to make sure she won a clapping contest. Val and I applauded enthusiastically for her, winning the contest for Rozetta. This wasn't hard—only three other people were attending. Rozetta knew how to dance seductively to music; the other dancer, though much shapelier, wasn't remotely in synch with the music. Rozetta won the fifty-dollar prize. Val and I expected her to buy us a watered-down drink (all they served) after the performance, but no such luck; she probably needed the money for her habit.

Drizza was daft as well. She collected disability payments from the government and kept her employment secret from them. Her bar was all off-the-books, I gathered. Supposedly, she was mentally impaired but the only time I got any sense of that was when she got strep throat—or something much worse. She had visited the commune and took a dare to eat off of a sick person's plate. Drizza believed she was living such a healthy lifestyle, and she was so spiritually pure, she couldn't possibly get sick. The bug thought otherwise. She was deathly ill when I left for California. I had helped her as best I could; the others in her crew were away. I ran cold baths for her and used a damp cloth to cool her fever down, but to no avail. She couldn't kick the sickness, didn't want to see a doctor, and wouldn't take anything but holistic medicine. Like that's going to help.

The trip to California? Yeah, it's coming. Don't worry. Chill. It was probably good that I left town. Drizza got another friend to come to my place—Drizza had sort of moved in—to take care of her. But Drizza became delirious with the fever, and her friend had the good sense to take her to a hospital where Drizza continued to refuse modern medicine. Finally, a doctor ignored her, gave her a shot of antibiotics, and saved her life. Drizza, of course, was furious. How dare that doctor disobey her instructions!

I've been skeptical of natural cures ever since.

I never had a lot of contact with Big Red. He was a huge guy, scarlet-haired with a bushy red beard, and prone to anger from time to time, unlike Drizza, Rozetta, and Black Robert, who were peaceful, spacey, relaxed people...when not being zany.

Big Red sold dope as near as I could make out, probably grown near the commune. He'd disappear for a while, then return with bags of weed. He'd smoke a bag in their room—yes, four in one room—before he began sharing with "friends," for a small fee.

Robert was called Black Robert to distinguish him from White Robert, another person living on the commune. I guess that worked in those days. He got his infamy from inadvertently getting into a shootout with a deranged guy visiting the commune. There was a standoff with shotguns in a cornfield, angry accusations exchanged, and shots fired. Afterwards, only Robert was standing. The court ruled it as self-defense. Nevertheless, he'd killed a man, giving him notoriety.

Robert was very upset about the incident and never talked about it, but everyone knew the story. To me, Robert was a gentle, caring soul; I couldn't imagine him harming a fly, but sometimes you gotta do what you gotta do.

One day, Robert came by my pad to tell me about a fabulous new album he had discovered: Charles Wright's *Rhythm and Poetry*. He'd heard it in the local record store and really dug it. Robert was excitedly explaining its merits when I pulled it out of a stack of LPs and put it on my turntable. That blew him away; he never expected me to have such an obscure jazz title. My street cred rose enormously. Of course, I had gotten the record from my dad, who owned a Country Western radio station and had no use for it, but I didn't tell Robert that. After that, Robert and I were buddies, and we'd play jazz, smoke dope, and talk late into the night; I must have given him the record because it disappeared from my life when I moved to London to study. I'm a firm believer in putting albums, books, etc., into the hands of people who genuinely cherish them.

On the album, Charles Wright sings "Here Comes the Sun." Dig it. You will know why it's an unknown album when you hear him.

That was the good yin group; the bad yang was straight across the hallway, a couple. They constantly argued and yelled at each other and one night came to blows. The walls were paper thin, and I could hear everything from across the hall; the commune tenants were away. So, I rapped on the door to urge them to stop. Fortunately, I was in my pajamas, and the guy decided I had a good reason for getting him to stop hitting his girlfriend; he assumed I wanted some quiet to get some sleep. But it was incredibly upsetting to listen to the brutality, so I complained to one landlord, whose only comment was "Why didn't you call the police?"

Well, we never called the cops because we didn't trust them. This hotshot knew that and wanted to rub it in my face. Nice guy. So, I had to deal with it myself. But I was lucky; they soon moved out.

One long weekend in spring, Drizza, Robert, Big Red, and Rozetta invited me to visit their commune. We all piled into Robert's Mercedes and headed south, traveling on old logging roads for the last ten miles to reach their settlement in the forest. The hamlet had many hand-built huts—some with elaborate verandas. There were vegetable gardens everywhere, and a field of newly planted corn. If I was interested, Drizza said, she would nominate me to be a member of the commune. Everything was decided by consensus or, sometimes, public votes. There were no secrets.

Some people were interesting. One person was a computer programmer and every year he'd leave the commune to work in San Jose on a coding project. He'd come back with big bucks and live the rest of the year doing whatever he wanted. Another was an artist and her work was startling and original, but it's a tough gig. No one had strong family ties; everyone was estranged from their biological families. Life was like that in the early days of hippiedom. The community was their family and, like all families, there was much squabbling and back-biting. The usual stuff. I helped with the gardening, the cooking and the cleaning up, but felt no genuine connection. The overall feeling I had was the same I felt for my work at the highway department: this is boring. Smoking dope, gardening, cooking, and telling tall tales wasn't particularly engaging. I never asked to be a member; commune living wasn't for me.

So, that was the life I was living, and the trip to California came as a welcome relief. Instead of hitchhiking, which was probably only safe in Oregon, I took the Greyhound. I don't remember much about the trip; I probably read, slept, and looked out the window when we passed through forests. But I remember arriving in Riverside at dusk. I found a pay phone and called Granddad Ike. My first shock of the trip was to learn Granddad was deaf. So, on the phone I spoke to his new wife, Betty, who informed me that my granddad did not drive at night; he'd pick me up in the morning. That was my second upset; where the hell was I supposed to stay?

I needed to find accommodation. I wasn't going to sleep outdoors near this conservative town; the last time I did that, it didn't work out so well. I was hitchhiking to Maine from my uncle's place on Long Island and needed a place to sleep for the night. I found a sandy place to snooze far outside of Provincetown because I'd heard there were issues in this area with sleeping in the open. But it wasn't far enough. I slept OK until the cops woke me up at 4:00 a.m. and took me to jail. I needed to pee badly but was too bashful to do it in the cell with another dozen young men and one toilet, no beds. After "breakfast"—a stale donut and cup of coffee that I did not drink because of my overloaded bladder—the cops took us to the judge, who was presiding in a long hallway. No fancy courtroom for us—we got the corridor. We all lined up, and the judge, sitting on a highchair behind an elegant podium blazoned with the city emblem, would say to each of us, "Five dollars or five days, what'll be?" After you paid, he'd pound his gavel on the podium and shout, "Next!" American justice in action. Hippies were not well liked in those days. Vagrant hippies, even less.

Fortunately, I had the five bucks, but the poor guy behind me didn't, so I lent him the money and gave him my temporary address (Val's place outside Kennett Square). And, by golly, he mailed me the cash a month later.

I asked around, and one of the Greyhound people pointed to a place across the street from the depot. Here's what I learned from this experience: never stay at a hotel near a bus depot. Duh.

I checked in, paid the nightly fee, and got a key to a room on the second floor. The hotel was not called the Sleazy Bus Depot Hotel; that would've been too apt; it was the Riverside Hotel, which sounded almost respectable until you saw the lobby and the chambers. The door to my room was flimsy and could easily have been pushed open with a heavy shoulder shove, so I put the fridge in front of the door to provide a little protection. It would at least give me a warning, should intruders try to enter. I'm not sure whether I was worried about my safety or my worthless possessions; maybe I was just agitated after the long ride.

The fridge was a small, ancient model with short iron feet. I walked it over to the door and looked around the room, satisfied I was reasonably safe. Where the icebox had been was a six-inch-high pile of dead cockroaches. They must have been spraying regularly to keep the roach population down and then sweeping the lifeless carcasses under the fridge. Talk about lazy housekeeping. Fortunately, there were no dead guys under the rickety twin-size bed, and I wasn't going to look under the dresser. Still, I shuddered from top to bottom when I crawled into bed.

I got some sleep, and the following day, after I phoned Granddad to remind him to pick me up, I found a diner for some food and coffee. I was thankful that the food was edible, but the coffee was the usual circa '74: brown water. About an hour later, he arrived, and I put my duffle bag on the back seat and piled into the front. Granddad Ike's cars were all Oldsmobiles because he owned some GM stock and loved the safety of these vehicles. This one was an Olds 98 with a Rocket 455 V-8 Turbo engine. A real beaut, but more powerful than necessary for the retirement community of Hemet, where golf carts were the popular mode of transportation.

Granddad greeted me by waving me into the car. In his youth, he was a big chunk of a man, tall and hefty. Now, he was shrunken with age, but still formidable, bald as a well-worn rock from a flowing stream with great hairy ears. We got underway, and Granddad got the big boat into the middle of the four-lane boulevard and headed toward the outskirts of town.

Only problem was...he was going the *wrong way* up the street.

I quickly fastened my seat belt while shouting, "We're going up a one-way street!" and motioning with my arm.

He couldn't hear a thing.

And paid no attention to my frantic hand signals.

All the cars coming at us were honking and swerving out of our way. Granddad had his elbow out the wide-open window, pipe in mouth, puffing away as calmly as you please, occasionally commenting on the weather, and totally unfazed by cars going the other direction, passing us on the left and right. I guess he wasn't even looking at the road.

We continued like that for ten blocks, at which point I was so slumped in my seat I could barely see out the windshield. But I couldn't take my eyes off the road; I was morbidly fascinated to see a head-on collision. Finally, we turned onto another roadway, fortunately going the correct direction, and found the highway to Hemet. Maybe the drivers in Riverside were accustomed to older folks cruising through in their Oldsmobiles. All I know is no vehicle even came close to hitting us, and some of them were quite gentle on their horns.

Granddad loved to play golf, but it gets tricky as one ages. Fortunately, Hemet had a nine-hole chip-and-putt course, the perfect way to spend the afternoon. I did my best but was pleased to see how happy Granddad Ike was when he touted up the final score with him ahead by a few strokes.

Here's how our discussion went while we were playing:

"It's a great day for playing golf," I'd say. "The weather is perfect."

"Yes, when you chip the ball to the green, you must make sure your club gets under it," Granddad would say, demonstrating with his nine iron on the grass.

"I got a five on that hole," I'd say.

"What was your score?"

"A five."

"Come again?"

I'd hold up my five fingers and mouth "five." No point saying it out loud.

At dinner, I quickly learned that my new step-grandma did not approve of me. It wasn't just my shoulder-length wavy hair, blue jeans, and flower-child shirt; there was something else, something deeper. Oh, she was polite enough, in a smug sort of way, but hardly friendly. I guess I kind of hoped she would be interested in getting to know Granddad's family. But there was none of that. And, of course, she was the only one I could talk to; Granddad couldn't hear, limiting our discussions to him talking and me nodding while listening to him.

The next day, I was grateful when my sister June and mom, Lizzie, arrived. Finally, I now had some friendly people to converse with. Betty showed June and me around the house. Walking in front of us, pointing out the spare bedrooms, the den, etc., with a wave of her hand, she passed a continuous stream of flatulence. The farts made a faint popping noise as she emitted them. June asked me if I thought Betty was aware of what she was doing, to which I replied, "Oh, she knows; she thinks we're gold diggers."

One night, we went to dinner with Betty's two sons, who arrived in separate cars so we could get to the restaurant in comfort. One son took Granddad, Lizzie, June, and me; the other drove his mom. Note: his mom traveled with none of us. I was in the front seat since I was the tallest, and I recounted my driving adventure with Granddad to Betty's oldest son, Garrison, who was driving. He laughed uproariously. He laughed so hard I thought we might get in an accident. How ironic would that have been, given Granddad and I had survived without the slightest scratch in Riverside? Granddad was in the back seat, oblivious. Mom and June also found it amusing, but only chuckled and shook their heads. The son's laughter told me what he and his brother thought of Granddad. Still, they were friendly to us, unlike their mother.

We arrived at the restaurant intact and arranged ourselves, as one might expect. Granddad was at the head of the table, with Betty to his left and Mom on his right. Betty's sons sat next to her, and June and I were on Mom's side of the table, across from the sons. We faced off, as if in a verbal hockey match, with Granddad as the referee.

After the salads arrived, Mom launched the first attempt at a goal, speaking loudly, hoping Granddad might hear. Fat chance. "I've secured funding to buy and renovate the old post office in Coos Bay, and we'll be able to move the Coos Art Museum into that building soon."

Betty, the goalie, stopped the shot with, "My older son, Garrison, just closed a merger deal at his bank worth twenty million dollars. I'm so proud of him."

Mom, with another shot at the goal, said, "We'll be the third largest art museum in Oregon after we complete the transition." She neglected to mention that there were only three such museums in all of Oregon.

"And my younger son, Barrett, just sold a home for one million dollars to a Hollywood star. Of course, we can't name the actor," said Betty, batting the puck into the middle of the rink.

"What do you do, Frank?" Garrison asked after seeing I had the puck.

"I just graduated from the University of Oregon with a degree in sociology and will work for the highway department this summer." Frank loses the puck. "But in the fall, I'll start a master's program in economics at the London School of Economics." Frank regains the puck and passes it to June.

"And I work in a shipping office doing the administrative work, making sure our clients' goods get to their destination."

"It was really cool working with the actor and finding him a home; he was chill," Barrett said, slamming the puck into the net.

Though Lizzie was normally quite good at one-upmanship, the game proceeded like this with the George family getting slaughtered by Betty and her sons.

At the end of the meal, Granddad, beaming and head nodding, concluded the match. "I'm pleased to see you all getting along so well."

On the way home to Oregon, I slept in the back seat; Lizzie and June shared the driving. After cruising into North Bend, I stayed a night, then hitched the next morning to Eugene to start my job as a surveyor assistant with the highway department.

So, what did I learn from my trip to see my granddad? Obviously, I couldn't communicate with him much—his hearing didn't allow for that. So, there was no poignant reunion. It was a failure that way, especially with my step-grandma viewing the visit as leaching on Granddad. But I learned from what didn't happen.

"You're on your own, kid," Granddad might have said, if he had known my wishes for stronger family ties. Then, he would have added, "Good luck."

THE RUN TO LESOTHO[1]

Instead of finding a quiet place in South Africa to bury the arms, I would do this run differently. My instructions were to take the shipment to Maseru, the capital of Lesotho, and connect with a local comrade there. We'd use code phrases to identify each other—some lines from a Nadine Gordimer novel, I gathered.

Job had said, "A comrade will find you in Maseru while you are window shopping and say: 'What are you doing here, Didier?' To which you reply, 'Perhaps you want to look at the flat anyway?'"

"That's kind of a weird thing to say. Are we sure we don't want to go with, 'The eagle has landed'?" I had replied.

"No, it is all set. We can't deviate from this now."

"OK, but how will they know to approach me?"

"Don't worry about it. We have given the contact your description."

I thought, OK, "tall White American guy with wavy hair pretending to be a tourist" would probably work. Anyway, it would have to do.

---

[1] This story is Chapter 21 in *Our Man in Mbabane: A Novel Based on a True Story*

On Saturday afternoon, I drove to Job and Michael's se-cluded place outside Manzini—in Swaziland where I lived and worked—to pick up the arms for this run. As always, they packed the car very efficiently, swiftly filling the small hiding space in my panel van behind the front seats. Even though I wasn't going to bury them this time, all the guns, ammo, and explosives were carefully bound in Bubble Wrap and tightly taped. It was 1979, and the military struggle against apart-heid was slowing gaining traction; the comrades on the front lines needed weapons.

"These are AK-47s," Job said, putting in five.

"And these are Scorpion pistols," said Michael, loading in five of those.

"This is ammunition, and these bricks are plastic explo-sives," Job said. "And don't worry," he assured me, "it takes a detonator to set this off, and those are in this separate package."

"That's a great comfort. Thanks."

"Here, give them this bag also," Job said. "They said they needed one." He threw an empty blue carryall into the back of the car.

"Sure. No problem."

"*Hamba kahle, bhuti* (Go well, brother)," Michael and Job said.

"*Sala kahle, bhutis* (Stay well, brothers)," I replied. With that, I got back in the van for the return up the hill to Mbabane. The eight-hour trip to Lesotho could wait until the next day.

I parked in front of my flat, which was at the top of a hill. Nothing ever seemed to happen to vehicles we parked near these expat homes, so the risk of leaving them there over-night seemed small.

Early the following day, after a hearty breakfast, I packed a lunch for the road. Having food would allow me to avoid stopping for a meal, interacting with others, and leaving my car unattended. After delivering the munitions, I could dine at my hotel in Ermelo, South Africa, on the route back to Swaziland.

I put my suitcase and lunch on the passenger seat and headed to the frontier. Passing through the Swazi border control at Ngwenya was easy—departing cars gather little attention. I parked on the South African side, walked into the Oshoek border post, and received my sticker and stamp in my passport, which had a proper visa. But before allowing me entry to South Africa, the guard glanced into the back of my panel van.

"What is in the bag?" he asked.

"It's empty. I'll use it for my shopping."

"Good. Welcome to South Africa."

I felt strange heading out of the country to deliver armaments to other comrades. I'd scouted out a place to bury the shipment on the four prior runs before returning later with the munitions. Those trips had been successful, with only one being rudely interrupted by some soldiers, so why change a winning strategy?

While driving toward Lesotho, I reflected on my nearly two years in Swaziland. This run was only my fifth for the African National Congress, Nelson Mandela's organization, so they were hardly overworking me. But I was conflicted. Getting these arms to the comrades in Lesotho this weekend made it impossible to meet with my girlfriend, Lindi. My disappointment of missed time with her dampened my enthusiasm for the gunrunning. Maintaining my "revolutionary fervor" when making so few trips to transport weapons was increasingly difficult.

The trip was quick and featureless. Though Swaziland and Lesotho have mountains, the road between them is in the Highveld of South Africa, a flat region stretching from one to the other. Brush, farms, and trees filled the landscape, broken up by the occasional town. The roads were well paved and straight, so it was an efficient and comfortable drive, if not a picturesque one.

I arrived at the border a little after 4:00 p.m. Getting through the frontier into Lesotho was no problem. The country needed tourists desperately. Its main export, by a wide margin, was labor to work in the South African mines. Money sent home by these workers sustained the country at the time. They weren't paid much for their demanding and dangerous work, were housed away from their families in crowded compounds where diseases spread quickly, and had to contend with their White managers' racism. Still, they preferred this to no work at all.

Being a tourist in a developing country can be difficult. Everyone wants to sell you something. To kill time, I carefully inspected everything offered in the Maseru shops, but quickly. A prolonged examination increased the expectation of a sale. I ended up buying a couple of small decorative wool weavings. Lesotho is famous for tapestries of village scenes, animals, and people.

An hour passed. What if no one ever came? What would I do? Drive back to Swaziland with the arms? It would be better to bury them here, document how to find them, and head out.

After all, this method had always worked previously. Why wasn't it the delivery process this time?

I continued to roam around, investigating the handicraft shops, having a cold drink at a café, keeping an eye on the car, and trying not to look suspicious. But the waiting was becoming stressful, and my aimless rambling was attracting occasional curious looks from tourists and shopkeepers. I'd never reached somewhere to deliver munitions without reconnoitering it before arriving. Now, strolling in the shopping area was becoming simultaneously tedious and tiring, especially with the necessity of monitoring my vehicle. I wanted to get rid of the guns as swiftly as possible, not dawdle.

Where's my contact?

As I wandered, an Afrikaner approached me. "Staying long in Lesotho?" he asked.

My immediate thought: *Is this a South African Police agent?*

"No, not long, just searching for some gifts for friends," I replied, my hair bristling at the back of my head.

"You're from Swaziland, eh?" he asked.

"Yes, how did you know?" I said, wondering how long he had been observing me.

"You are keeping a careful eye on it," he said, flicking his head toward my parked van.

"Yes, you can never be too careful," I said.

"Yah, you can't trust these kaffirs. They're a sneaky lot," he said, smiling and nodding.

I chose not to reply, but just observed him. He certainly looked like an SAP officer. Tall and heavyset, he had sandy hair and a ruddy face. He appeared to have gotten a slight sunburn recently; his cheeks were bright pink. His clothes were a standard Afrikaner outfit: a short-sleeved shirt with a pocket, green slacks, and heavy brown shoes.

"Searching for gifts, you say?"

"Yes," I said.

He looked around at the shops and parked vehicles, then his gaze returned to me, his eyes sharply focused on my face.

What's this guy's game? I thought, my palms perspiring.

"I'm here alone," he said. "I thought you might like to go for a drink."

"Thanks, but I'm meeting someone for dinner. I'm not sure where he is, but I'm sure he'll be here soon."

"Ach," he said. "OK. I thought I saw a friendly face."

With that, he left and headed toward a hotel where I'm sure he found a bar. If he was SAP, I couldn't tell; maybe he was just lonely.

My stomach was still in knots when, finally, after an interminable two hours, someone approached me and said the Didier line. I replied with the comment on the flat.

He grinned broadly. "Where did you park?"

"Not far. Just over there."

"OK. Let's go."

We walked to the car and climbed in. "Where to?" I asked.

"Take this road out of town, and I will direct you from there."

We headed out of Maseru and drove for about twenty minutes until we reached a quiet road that ended at a cluster of small buildings at the top of a hill.

Four more comrades approached the car, which made me nervous. How many comrades were going to meet me? I recalled my original recruitment conversation with Walter, where he explained that everyone who is caught breaks under torture and talks. A real pep talk. Now here I was, meeting some trained soldiers from our side. A first for me, but a risk.

They all introduced themselves, we shook hands, and they began to pepper me with questions.

"You are American. I can tell from your accent."

"Yes."

"What is your name?"

"Polo."

"That's a funny name. What is your real name?"

"Polo."

"What state are you from?"

"Oregon."

"Oregon? That's on the West Coast, eh?"

"Yes."

"You're so tall. Did you play basketball at school?"

"No, I wasn't good at that."

I thought, *Oh, great. A tall, White guy from Oregon, driving a beige Toyota Corolla panel van with Swazi plates, who can't play basketball. That nails me right there. It would be so easy to track me down. I hope none of these guys ever gets caught by the South African Police.*

They'd be safe if the Afrikaners arrested me. Their names were already a blur. I'd never recollect how to get to this spot and would have difficulty describing them as well. Not impressive in many ways, but helpful in this case.

Toughen up, Polo.

"Where are the munitions?" one of the comrades asked.

I moved the van seats forward and began to unscrew the panel plate with the screwdriver from the glove box while they watched from both sides of the car. When I took the panel out and laid it on the platform, they spotted the packages, pushed me aside, and began pulling everything out.

"Wow. This is great. This car is nice. Who found it?"

"I did."

"Super selection! Look at all these AK-47s and pistols!"

They unwrapped the packages and began examining the rifles and pistols.

The ANC had trained them, probably in Namibia or Mozambique, to use these weapons and make bombs. They handled the guns professionally. I hadn't seen one unwrapped before; all I'd ever held were the swathed packages. One comrade handed me an AK-47, which I aimed at a nearby tree. Aside from BB guns, my only experience with guns was a .22 rifle. My dad had taught me to use the one he owned. He grew up on a farm and used it to shoot rabbits in their fields. Once, in the Boy Scouts, I won an ice cream cone for being the best shot in my small troop. My knowledge was limited to carefully aiming and slowly pulling the trigger, the total extent of my "military" training. These comrades would face an enemy much more formidable than a paper target. I silently wished them well for their upcoming missions.

"Join us for dinner! We should celebrate, *bhuti!*" one said.

"No, I have to get back," I said. "I can't stay."

"Don't say that," another said. "You can leave tomorrow."

"Unfortunately, I have a nine a.m. meeting at work tomorrow in Mbabane. I also need to stop on the way back and get some wine for my cover—to explain where I was this weekend." Hopefully, something would still be open in Ermelo.

"You like wine?" a comrade said. "These Boers know how to make wine, eh?"

"Yes, they certainly do," I replied.

It would've been fun to stay with them and hear about their exploits and plans to the extent they could speak of them. But the less I knew about them and their procedures, and they knew about me and mine, the better. I had expected to meet only one comrade and have him unload the car with me at a secluded place. I never anticipated a welcoming party. But they were comfortable living here and had no worries about being observed.

I screwed the panel back into place, and we said our goodbyes. At the last moment, the carryall bag in the back caught my eye.

"Oh, hey. I was supposed to give you this."

I grabbed the bag and started to hand it to one of them. Something in it was rattling, so I opened it to see what it was. My stomach sank as I remembered the time when my bag had been randomly searched on my first run into South Africa. Rolling at the bottom of the bag was a single bullet for an AK-47.

ISLANDS

Fucking Kiawah Island again, Andrea thought. *Couldn't they come up with somewhere else for once?*

Her family had been going to the same vacation place each summer since she was eight years old. The beach was pleasant, and you could ride a bicycle from one end of the island to the other, but that grew tiresome after two days. She had agreed to stay for five nights, cutting her time with her family short, but it would still feel like an eternity.

She was arriving two days later than the rest of her family. Her parents and brother had probably already slipped into a comfortable routine, which she felt would exclude her. Her father seemed equally detached from his children, but she wondered why her mother favored her brother. Andrea was the successful one. She had excelled in math at school and now was a trader with a large Wall Street bank. Andrea was swimming in lucre. Her bonuses were obscene, but she deserved them. She worked hard for her firm, and they profited from her trading skills. And she had to put up with all the shit from her male colleagues.

Frank had none of that. He was a poet who worked as a bartender to make a living, a cliché if there ever was one. Yes, he had published one slim volume of poetry and did well at some of the New York poetry slams, but really—what had he accomplished? Like her, he was still unmarried, but unlike her, he dated successfully. Well, of course, he was a heterosexual bartender in New York. How hard could it be to find a date when you're serving beautiful, single, sometimes desperate women every night? In contrast, she could not hold on to a relationship. All her male colleagues at work unequivocally wanted trophy wives, not someone independent, assertive, and alpha. All the dating apps seemed to supply only wimps and clones of her colleagues, nothing in between.

Occasionally, Frank would bring his latest squeeze to Kiawah, but—fortunately—he wasn't dating anyone significant lately. The last one, Angela, had garnered so much attention, Andrea had felt invisible to her parents, who cooed endlessly over Angie. So what if she was knock-down, drop-dead gorgeous, and always Pollyannaish? She had the brain of an acorn. With that IQ, she couldn't be a trophy wife, so she was stepping up big-time to date a pretentious poet, masquerading as a bartender.

Andrea's limo delivered her late on Monday morning, but her dad Eugene had waited to prepare breakfast, which included *crêpes*—Andrea's favorite—until she got there. Her mother, Laura, greeted her warmly with a hug, while Eugene waved nonchalantly and rubbed her back before returning to the stove. Frank looked up from his book and beamed a megawatt, blinding-white smile her way. He was handsome. And he knew it.

"How was your trip down, honey?" Laura asked Andrea.

"Just fine," Andrea replied. "The plane was on time, and the limo was waiting for me."

"That's lovely," Laura said. "I'm so happy you can afford limos. I'm very proud of how well you are doing at work."

"We're both very proud," Eugene said as he flipped the first *crêpe*.

"Thanks, Mom. Thanks, Dad. It's hard work, but I enjoy it."

"I wish I understood how you made so much money just buying and selling securities," Laura said.

"It's not complicated," Andrea replied. "I buy low and sell high."

"Yes, but where does the money come from?" Laura asked.

"I've explained it before. Right now, I'm starving."

"Here you go," Eugene said, placing the first *crêpe* on Andrea's plate. Andrea sprinkled powdered sugar on it, squeezed a lemon half over it, and began eating.

Frank rose from the sofa to join his mother and sister at the table. The second *crêpe* landed on his plate shortly thereafter.

"No girlfriend this time?" Andrea asked her brother.

"I'm taking a break from dating and concentrating on my next book of poems," Frank said.

"Oh, what's it about?" Laura asked. "Tell us, dear. Can you read us one of your poems?"

"It's a set of apocryphal stories of love, but I haven't completed any yet, and I don't like to share unfinished poems."

"Why not about genuine liaisons?" Andrea asked. "You've had many," she added, trying to be subtle.

"*Touché*," Frank said. "Perhaps I've been reflecting on your dating experiences."

"Stop it, you two," Laura said. "We have only all just come together. This is family time. Please try to be civil to one another."

Eugene had been busy and arrived at the table with a stack of *crêpes*. *"Bon appetit!"* he said as he sat down. "More, Frank, please. Have you found a publisher? How many poems will the book include?"

"The volume is somewhat inchoate at present," Frank said. "I have put out some feelers to a couple of publishers, but they want to see the finished pieces. They'd also love it if I had many of them published in a variety of literary journals."

"How convenient that your work is still so undeveloped," Andrea said.

"Andrea, that's enough!" Laura said. "You're sniping will be the death of me."

"Unlikely, but duly noted," Andrea replied.

"In any case, I'm happy with the progress I've made so far," Frank said. "I like a lot of the ideas and phrasing I have in my drafts."

"We look forward to reading it when you finish it," Eugene said. "Laura and I thoroughly enjoyed your first volume. You liked it too, didn't you, Andrea?"

"They're good poems, but the big-city angst theme was not my cup of tea," Andrea said.

"Too close to home?" Frank asked.

"Too banal," Andrea replied.

"Ouch," Frank said.

"What have you been doing on your weekends, Andrea?" Laura asked.

"Do you mean, have I been dating someone? The answer is 'no.' I'm pretty tired from work, but I go to yoga classes and see my friends for drinks or meals."

"You look fit," Eugene said.

"I stay in shape. It helps me think clearly at work. I try to exercise as often as possible."

"You look great," Frank said.

"Thanks," Andrea said, arching one eyebrow as she gazed at her brother.

Andrea looked at the fish and felt empty. She'd never much enjoyed eating them, but Dad loved to buy fresh-caught shark, bass, and redfish. They were at a roadside stall, the angler proudly displaying his morning catch on a bed of ice which was melting rapidly. It was morning, but already the heat was oppressive on the mainland. The humidity drenched your clothes no matter how thin the fabric, making it cling to your body. A half-hearted breeze only made you wish for a stronger wind.

Dad selected a redfish, his favorite. He'd cook it on the grill with corn and zucchini. Mom would slice ripe peaches, dust them in powdered sugar, and they'd have that for dessert with ice cream.

It's so fucking conventional! Like we're an ordinary family.

They spent the rest of the day doing the usual island things—bike ride in the morning, sunbathing and reading in the afternoon, a drink while the grill warmed up. This unit had a Weber grill requiring charcoal. Dad had selected some with hickory in it. Andrea had to admit it smelled divine, like a smoky hug from a giant teddy bear.

"I'll have a gin and tonic," Andrea said. Frank always acted as the family bartender; after all, it was his profession. "With a twist of lime."

"Twist or a slice?" Frank asked.

"You're right. I meant a slice," Andrea said, her forehead tightly knit, her mouth a frown.

"Thanks. It's easier. Dad. Mom. What will you be drinking?"

"A white wine would be lovely. I'm sure your dad will have the same. I'll take it to him," Laura said as she exited the living room to the back porch.

"And I'll have the same as you, Andrea," Frank said. "It's refreshing after the heat from the sun, the sand, the humidity."

"Do you always have to speak as if you're reciting a poem?"

"I aspire to be a poet, so I practice whenever I can. Do you think a lot about your trades and the markets?"

"After the markets close and I turn off my terminal, I try to shut it all out. I'll go to a yoga class or for a run."

"I collapse in a heap after work. It's physically demanding being on your feet all evening and emotionally draining dealing with the customers. It's a performance; I can understand why so many actors do it in between gigs."

"Or do it as their permanent gig."

"Yes, not many can make a living as an actor. Or poet," Frank said, laughing.

"I don't know why you even try; wouldn't it be smarter and more lucrative to get a real job—something with potential for advancement?"

"It may come to that. But, for now, I'm giving it a few more years. My dream is to teach creative writing at a small college."

"Ugh. I can't imagine anything more horrid. You'd be trading your drinking customers for students. I'm not sure that's a step up."

"Fair point. But I'd have a lot more time for my writing." Frank topped up their depleted glasses with gin, tonic, and a couple of ice cubes.

"And what makes you think a college would hire you?"

"Don't tell Mom and Dad, but I'm enrolled in an MFA program."

"Huh," Andrea said, scrunching her eyebrows in surprise.

"Dinner is ready!" Laura said, entering the living room and putting a large platter of fish and vegetables on the dining table. Like most beach houses, the kitchen, living room and dining area were all in one large space.

They sat down, with Eugene at one end and Laura opposite him. Frank and Andrea sat across from each other.

"Frank tells me he is taking an MFA course," Andrea said, before taking a bite.

"Yes," Frank said, glaring at Andrea.

"That's wonderful!" Laura said. "I'm so happy for you. Are the courses interesting?"

"I'm enjoying them."

"He hopes to teach creative writing at a college someday," Andrea said, with only a hint of derision.

"Yes, that's the plan," Frank said, attempting to stab his sister with his eyes.

"How long have you been in the program?" Eugene asked.

"About a year. I'm taking it part time, so I've finished one-quarter of the two-year course. I was going to tell you earlier but was waiting for an opportune time."

"Well, I propose a toast to the successful completion of your master's degree and the job of your dreams," Eugene said, lifting his wineglass high in the air.

"Yes, cheers," Laura said, lifting her glass. Andrea was silent but lifted her glass, tilted her head, and cocked an eyebrow.

"Again, we have Frank as the center of attention," Andrea said. "I've always thought you favored him over me."

"Dear, you brought up his studies," Laura said in as hard a voice as she could muster. "And we love you both equally."

"Mmm. My bonus this year was three hundred thousand dollars. Better than nearly all my fellow traders. But I never feel you care about me or my successes."

"We love you and we want you to be happy," Laura said.

"Yes, we care about you; not the money you make," Eugene said, pouring himself another glass of wine. He offered the bottle to Laura, who was nodding at his comment, but shook her head at the wine.

"Do you?" Andrea said. "I wonder."

"We do care," Laura said. "But you often seem sad, sometimes angry, and that worries us."

"You don't worry about me. I can still remember the time I tripped Frank and he cut his knee. You and Dad practically accused me of attempted murder. It was an accident!"

"We may have overreacted," Eugene said. "It was a nasty cut on a piece of glass, and we were upset and didn't know if we could stop the bleeding."

"Well, I didn't understand that then. I was six years old!"

"Andrea, why are you bringing this up now?" Laura asked. "This is so far in the past."

"I don't know!" Andrea said. "I just feel unloved." She burst into tears, stood up and looked around for a tissue. Laura rose and moved to hug her, but Andrea dodged her and headed for a box of Kleenex on the kitchen counter. Laura walked over and rubbed her back; Andrea shirked away.

"The fish is superb, Dad," Frank said. "Cooked to perfection."

"Thank you, son."

"Come back to the table, Andrea," Laura said. "You've hardly had a bite."

"Yes, come back," Frank said. "I'm terribly impressed with your bonus; it's four times what I make in a year."

Andrea shook her head, blew her nose, but her family could see the faintest of smiles creasing her face.

"I'm sorry," Andrea said. "I must be stressed out from work. I'm exhausted."

"Eat your dinner," Laura said. "You'll feel better."

"I hate fish," Andrea said.

"I'll make you a burger," Eugene said, leaping up and heading for the kitchen.

"No, no, that's OK."

"Not a problem at all. I'm sure the fire is still hot."

While Eugene cooked, Laura and Frank talked about the weather, what they would do the next day and how much they enjoyed the corn and zucchini. Andrea tried the fish but could only get one bite down. For the rest of the evening, she was subdued, mostly nodding at the surrounding conversation. She ate all of her burger after Eugene presented it to her with a flourish.

Andrea struggled through the days of sunbathing, biking, and—for her—the insufferable family meals. Although she tried to be friendly and cordial, she found Frank's cheerfulness, her father's remoteness, and her mother's insistent pleasantness unbearable. The unclouded weather and heavy humidity did not help. She used her ultra-dark glasses to protect herself from both the sun's glare and her mother's probing questions about her dating life, or lack thereof.

Why do I bother? she asked herself. She lasted three days, then rearranged her flight and sent for a car. Each of her family gave her a goodbye hug after the vehicle pulled up. Then, they helped her load her luggage and blew her kisses.

Could it be me? Andrea thought as she stepped into the limousine.

NIGHTSHADE

"Do you mean I'm fired?" Edmund asked his boss, Clive Stanway.

The day had started like any other workday. Edmund had risen early, fed his cat, Chloe, exercised, and walked to work from his home in the Logan Square neighborhood of Philadelphia. It was a pleasant early summer day, sunny and not yet humid. Edmund's walk was a brisk fifteen minutes door-to-door, and the lovely weather put a spring into his step. While striding, he remembered how, as a child, he was so good at skipping great distances, outpacing his playmates in races.

Edmund worked as an accountant for a company that owned restaurants. He knew some of the dining places were performing poorly and had thought it a mistake to open an expensive one near Rittenhouse Square. There were already many great eateries there, and the competition was challenging, but Clive had insisted his place would be a huge success. It wasn't. However, knowing the finances of his company did not prepare him for that Friday morning. A note on his desk summoned him to Clive's office.

"Good morning, Ed," Clive said. "Have a seat." Edmund had long ago given up on asking people to call him by his full forename, though he preferred it.

"What can I do for you, Mr. Stanway?"

Edmund regarded his boss. Though coeval, he always thought of Clive as significantly junior to him in age. Perhaps it was Clive's supercilious nature. Clive was always quick with decisions and utterly confident in them, despite making many major misjudgments over the years. He treated with disdain anyone who raised an objection or provided a contrary viewpoint. Though often wrong, he was haughty, arrogant, and never doubted the truth of his vision.

"Unfortunately, I have been forced to declare my firm bankrupt," Clive said. "Covid has killed it. I am letting you go immediately. Here is your final paycheck." He passed a handwritten check to Edmund.

In response to Edmund's question, Clive said, "No. No. No. You are not being fired. You have done your job. It's just that your position no longer exists. Everyone will be let go, and all the restaurants closed. You can clear out your office and take your things home."

Never one to fulminate, usually calm and professional, Edmund struggled to say anything coherent. "But the business is not doing that badly," he blurted.

"It's over; I've decided to close everything down. Don't make this emotional."

Stunned, Edmund picked up his check, stood, stretched his head toward the ceiling to bring himself to his full five-foot-eight-inch height, nodded at Clive, turned, and left the office. On his way to his room across the hall, he noticed what he had not seen earlier. Clara, Clive's long-suffering assistant, was not at her desk. Moreover, there were no photos on it. Clara was married with two charming young children, who sometimes came to the office. She adored showing visitors their photos. She must have been informed the evening before when he was closing the books for May. Clive would have told her not to disturb Edmund on her way out of the office.

Edmund sat at his desk and began putting his belongings into his briefcase. Unmarried and childless, he had only a few beloved pens, an aging calculator, and one paperweight to take home. The walls had several posters he had put up to alleviate the drabness of the office, but he had no use for them at home. Before he left, he quickly checked the company's cash account on his computer. It was empty; his check would bounce.

Edmund stopped at his bank on his way home and waited patiently in line to see his favorite teller. When it was his turn, he approached her and said, "Jessie, I seem to have a problem."

"What's that, Mr. Baker?" Jessie asked, concern clouding her face.

"I don't believe there are any funds in this account to cash my paycheck," he said, pushing the check and deposit slip through the slot in the glass separating them.

"Let me see," she said. The restaurant business banked here as well.

"You're right," she said, after looking up the company's account on her terminal. "Its balance is zero. Is something wrong?"

"Yes, the firm is bankrupt, and I have been let go. Clive told me this morning and gave me this last check."

"Oh, I am so sorry to hear that. You certainly didn't deserve that, Mr. Baker."

"Thank you," he said. "You're very kind."

"Please leave this here with me, and I will check the company's account from time to time. If some new receivables appear in it, I'll cash and deposit your check when there are sufficient funds."

"I would greatly appreciate that," Edmund replied. "I may need it."

Though he had saved diligently over the years, Edmund was far from wealthy. He lived a comfortable but simple life, occasionally splurging on a vacation to the Caribbean in winter or an extravagant meal. At age sixty-four, he realized he was unlikely ever to get another full-time job. Who would want a highly experienced accountant when they could have a young, less costly one? Yes, he could use this last paycheck. He'd take himself to an expensive restaurant, somewhere he had never been.

Chloe was happy to see him and came running to greet him when he opened the door at home. He fed her a treat of roasted turkey, and she looked at him quizzically. Did she know it was unusual for him to be home on Friday morning? Cats seemed to know much more than we credit them. Chloe always knew how to get attention when she wanted it and stop it when she didn't. She was a pro at food requests. She was a house cat, so she did not need to know how to ask to go outside, but he was sure she would have learned if necessary. Aside from Chloe, Edmund was also fond of his two orchids. One was still blooming after five months. They sat on the windowsill with the most sunlight. He gave them an ice cube each, though they didn't need one.

What to do? Edmund was at a loss. Work provided grounding, a purpose in life, structure. He would need to arrange his affairs for retirement. Meanwhile, he had most of a Friday ahead of him. Shouldn't he be happy?

To keep himself busy, he would bring forward all his chores from Saturday. He could review his finances later. But first, a walk.

Edmund enjoyed walking. He prided himself on his ability to live in the city without a vehicle, and it kept him fit. As he stepped out of his front door, he noticed the foxgloves on his neighbor's stoop were blooming. Weren't they a poisonous plant?

He walked to Reading Terminal and picked up a large steak, potatoes, broccoli, and a baguette. On his way home, he picked up a bottle of Malbec, the most expensive on the shelf, at his local wine shop. He put all these things away in his kitchen, each in their proper place.

He sat at his dining table and began making a list of pros and cons. On the left side, he put Chloe, Orchids, and Meal at a Fine Restaurant. Then, he added: Charity Work: Helping small businesses with their accounts?; and Hobby: Painting? On the right side, he could only think of a question: What is the point?

He got on his computer and looked up foxgloves to learn how poisonous they were: toxic but not very deadly. If ingested, they could be fatal, but the irregular heartbeat, upset stomach, and confusion they caused sounded unpleasant. Then he researched nightshade. He liked the ring of the word. It was also called deadly nightshade, devil's cherry, and best of all, belladonna. Like the other plant, it had beautiful flowers, and it appeared to be more noxious than foxgloves. It also had particularly lethal berries: consuming ten to twenty could be fatal for adults. It was supposed to be one of the most toxic plants in the Western Hemisphere. However, the symptoms after eating the roots, leaves and berries were nasty—blurred vision, loss of balance, hallucinations, and convulsions.

Later, he went to the dry cleaners to pick up his shirts. He passed the homeless man on the corner of Market Street who always politely asked for spare change, and to which he replied, "Sorry." At least this person wasn't truculent like some beggars. But Edmund preferred to give to the local food banks; then, he knew people were getting nutrition and not buying cigarettes and booze with his donated money.

"It's Friday, Mr. Baker," Amy said anxiously as Edmond entered the shop. "What are you doing here?"

"I've retired," he replied, but the phrase sounded odd to him. "Today was my last day of work."

"Congratulations!" she said, with a huge, beaming smile.

"Thank you," he said, and he almost felt good, but he winced at the memory of his talk with Clive. Thirty years of doing his accounting ledgers and nothing but a dubious one-month paycheck to show for it. *The perfidious swine*, Edmund thought, startling himself with his sudden anger.

While walking back to his row house, his shirts folded over his left arm, he stopped at the iron fence protecting the Mütter Museum's garden and gazed through the bars. The shrubbery was spectacularly green and lush, and some plants sported flowers of various hues. An early-blooming hibiscus had large trumpet blooms of fiery red, changing to orange, then yellow at its outer edges. There were several plants with florets of yellow or white. Whoever maintained the garden made sure every plant was healthy, with robust foliage and blossoms. The gardeners had thoughtfully placed every stone on the small path that wound through the shrubbery. Even those stones covered with moss seemed to be intentionally chosen. The benches look comfortable and inviting. How had he never noticed this before? He had walked by this garden, an emerald oasis, once a week for decades. He hadn't been to the museum since he was a teenager. The deformed fetuses in formaldehyde and the skeletons were more interesting to him in those days. He decided to visit the museum and learn more about the plants in its tiny park.

At home, Edmund purchased a ticket for the museum and printed it. Then he left for the Mütter, only a few blocks away, taking his mask with him. Upon entering, Edmund refreshed his childhood memories by taking a quick tour of the permanent collection. It looked much the same as he recalled from his youth, lots of grim evidence of disease, often modeled in wax, deformed babies, skulls, etc. However, the special exhibit was about the influenza pandemic of 1918 and its impact on the city. Planned since 2015, there was a video commemorating the 17,500 deaths in Philadelphia attributed to the disease, made in September 2019. How prescient!

But he was impatient to see the garden, so he left the exhibit and exited the building. The heat of the day hit him like a large feather. It had been cooler inside than he realized. To his left, a brightly blossoming tree caught his eye. Behind it, ivy crept up the side of the building. The church facing him loomed over the garden, framing the park on the south side. He descended the steps to review the plants.

Many were medicinal. Marigold was good for infected wounds, swollen glands, and skin disease. Thyme helped with chest infections, bronchitis, colds, and flu. Wild ginger relieved digestive spasms. The sweet scent of an unidentified flower tickled his nose. There were many other plants as well, but no nightshade that he could find.

Edmund walked the length of the garden, about a hundred feet, and sat on a bench with shade near the iron bars. It was peaceful and serene. The bustle of the city felt far away. Even the sounds of cars driving by on Twenty-Second Street seemed distant.

He would plant a garden!

What should he plant? He toured the small space again, seeking inspiration for his garden. Perhaps some hibiscus; they were so beautiful. Maybe a few carnivorous pitcher plants, to reduce the number of insects. Definitely some chamomile—he could brew his own tea! Since he enjoyed cooking, he would have an area devoted to herbs. He liked the idea of perennial wildflowers also; color was always heartening, and wildflowers were hardy. A tree or two for shade would be pleasant as well. Currently, his small backyard was simply a patio of bricks. He would dig them up and replace them with topsoil. This project would give his life structure while he contemplated what to do in his remaining years.

His phone was ringing when he got home. It was Jessie from the bank. One of his firm's bistros had recently deposited last week's receipts; she had deposited his last paycheck into his account. *What a gem that Jessie is!*

He sat again at his dining table and glanced at his earlier list. Setting it aside for later contemplation, he started another list for his garden: hibiscus, azaleas, chamomile, pitcher plant, wildflowers, herbs, trees, and other bushes from a nursery.

Satisfied, he turned on his computer and ordered the wildflower and herb seeds. He would research nurseries in the area tomorrow.

Before turning off his computer, he hesitated, and then he also ordered some nightshade seeds.

Options are always good, he thought.

But for now, I'm going to focus on my garden. The best thing about options: you don't have to do them.

DELUGE IN ZURICH

Craig Cole buzzed Audrey's apartment but got no response. The heavy wind splashed the rain off his slicker, soaking his long legs. He buzzed it again. Hearing nothing but the splashing of cars in the street behind him, he pulled out a metal instrument from his jacket and picked the lock with his left hand. He entered the building, shut the door, and took off his shoes. Taking two steps at a time, he mounted the stairs to the top-floor residence. The door to the flat was slightly ajar, so he pushed it open and walked in, closing the door behind him with his elbow.

Craig put on gloves and, to reduce the stench from the room, a surgical mask. He groped for the light switch and winced when the lights flooded the apartment. Audrey, one of his CIA colleagues, was hanging from the banister, a noose around her neck. Dead.

The unit was a high-ceiling studio with a staircase to a loft sleeping area. The kitchen to the right had a small table with two chairs in front of it. A sofa, its back to the kitchen, was in the middle of the room, facing a wall-mounted TV near the door. The coffee table in front of the couch was undisturbed, but its side table was missing something. Craig looked under the settee and found a small chip of pottery with the same shade of blue as the table lamp, which formerly perched on the end table. He remembered it now from the time he dropped by for a drink with Audrey after work.

Craig approached Audrey's lifeless form and lifted her right hand to inspect her nails. Skin and specks of blood were under her unpolished fingernails. Her arm was heavy, limp, and lifeless. He lifted his hand to her head, turned her face toward the light, and inspected the bruises on her cheeks and forehead. Even through his rubber gloves, he could feel the chill of her skin. Craig's features tightened as he pursed his lips and let out a deep breath.

"Goodbye, Audrey."

"So, what did you see, Craig?" Marshall, Craig's boss, barked from behind a large desk, his hands flat on its surface. Their CIA office was in the American consulate of Zurich, in a quiet neighborhood on the east side of the lake. When the rain splashed against the window behind Marshall's head, they had to raise their voices to hear each other.

"It wasn't suicide. She had bruises around her face, and there was skin and blood under her fingernails. There probably was a struggle and someone cleaned up; I found a chip of a lamp under the sofa."

"She was sloppy," Marshall said.

"She was a good agent. I learned a lot from her. And she didn't deserve to die."

"Drop the sentimental crap. We can't afford to have feelings in this business," Marshall said, shaking his head, pushing back from his desk, and throwing his hands in the air. "That's the second agent we've lost in as many months. The Russkies must really be worried about our operations here." Becoming thoughtful, he asked, "How's that girlfriend of yours? She's not living with you, is she?"

"No, she's not," Craig said, but facing Marshall's intense stare, added, "She doesn't know anything; I never tell her about what I do."

"I hope not. She makes me nervous. You're too gullible; you always think the best of everyone."

"Her background check was clean."

"No one's clean," Marshall said, grabbing a piece of paper off his desk. "Anyway, we're ready to move."

"You know which safe deposit box is being used for the drop?" Craig asked, his eyes widened as he lifted his brows.

"We've narrowed it down to three." Marshall handed the sheet to Craig. "Memorize them."

Craig studied the numbers for a few seconds, then passed it back.

"You'll need to go in tonight. And don't fuck up. I don't want to bail you out of jail. Again! Twice was one time too many."

Craig recalled when he was in jail for the first time, seated at a table wearing an orange jumpsuit. He'd gotten caught on a safecracking job in the US and was doing time in a federal prison. His handcuffed wrists were resting on the table in the middle of an interrogation room. Two agents, both in dark suits, sat opposite him.

"We're offering you an early way out of jail," one agent said. "You'll just need to crack safes for us when we tell you to."

"Why me?" Craig asked.

"Because you're the best. You won the international safe-cracking competition two years in a row."

"We'll pay you a decent salary, and you'll get a new identity—you can start a whole new life," the other agent said. "You'll have to keep your nose clean, however."

"And if you don't accept our offer," the first agent interjected, "I'm sure we can find a way to make your life here even more miserable."

"Thanks. I appreciate that," Craig said, deadpan.

"Well, what do you say?"

"Sounds like an offer I can't refuse."

Craig shook his head to escape the memory and said, "I'm eternally grateful to you for springing me from jail in the US, but that time in Geneva was just bad luck. A pigeon tripped the alarm just as I was leaving the building."

"Whatever. It was hellish getting the Swiss authorities to keep everything quiet."

"Sorry, boss. But the mission was successful. I got the goods and delivered them to you. Even the Swiss didn't know what I was doing."

"I later heard something else was missing."

"I didn't take that."

"What's the saying? Once a thief..."

"I've gone legit."

"Yeah. Sure." Marshall paused, swiveling in his chair. "This time you'll need to leave no trace. We don't want anyone to know that we have the information on the Dmitry's Group armament shipments. Understood?"

"Understood," Craig said.

"Good." Marshall bounced his fingers on his desk like he was playing piano chords. "Take your gun."

"You know I never take it when I'm cracking safes. It's bad luck."

"I know, but it's dangerous out there. Take your gun."

"Whatever you say." Craig turned and headed to the door to leave.

"And Craig?" Marshall called out to Craig's back.

"Yes?"

"Don't get unlucky this time."

Craig stopped at the door, its knob in his hand, looking back at Marshall, expressionless. Then he turned and walked out.

Stanislav paced the conference room in the Russian embassy in Bern, where their foreign intelligence agency, SVR, had its offices. Bookshelves with bursting folders filled three walls of the room, lit only by a single, bare bulb. Misha, a large hulk of a man, sat at the table in the middle of the space, reviewing documents.

"That's two down, but we need the third one to crack the safe for us," Stanislav said. "You'll need to get his phone and camera from him. We need to know what our own paramilitaries are up to. Do we know when he is making his move?"

Misha grunts. "We're pretty sure. I have a hunch anyway."

"What's our undercover agent say?"

"I'll confirm this afternoon. Meanwhile, I'll travel to Zurich in case their operation is this evening."

"In this weather?"

"It's perfect weather. No one will be on the streets."

"Good." Stanislav said. "Get the information and kill him."

"Understood."

In the late afternoon, Craig entered his apartment block and took the elevator to his third-floor flat. His cat, Pud, greeted him with a meow. His girlfriend, Rosaria, a tall Italian with short-cropped blond hair, was standing in the middle of the living room/kitchen area, wringing her hands.

"Rosaria. You're home early," Craig said while scratching Pud's ear.

"I didn't sleep well last night and couldn't work, so I came home. I need to rest, but I feel too anxious."

"Anxious? What about?"

"I worry about you. I never know what you are doing or where you are."

"What I do is routine," Craig said, sighing. "I work for the US State Department, writing reports on the Swiss economy so the ambassador can be well-informed. Sometimes, I travel to get a better understanding of what's happening in a certain industry. What could be more boring?" Craig took off his dripping wet coat and hung it on a standing coat rack. Lightning from the window lit the room and was followed quickly by a crack of thunder.

"This rain. I'm so sick of this downpour. Won't it ever stop?" Rosaria said, holding her arms out. "Hold me."

Craig crossed the room and folded Rosaria into his arms. The cat rubbed his leg while he held Rosaria.

"There, there, no need to be upset. They say the rain will stop by morning." Craig kissed Rosaria, but she pulled away and sat on the edge of the sofa.

"I sense you are in danger and could be hurt. I don't know what I'd do without you."

"Why would you think that? Nothing I ever do is dangerous." He sat on the sofa, rubbed her back, and kissed her cheek. Craig's comforting words didn't sound reassuring even to him.

"The rain is unnerving us both," Craig said, hoping to hide the quaver in his voice. "We just need some rest." Craig continued to rub Rosaria's back. "Hey. I'm really sorry, but I just came home to pick up a few things. I have to leave town on short notice, and I won't be back until late. Probably after midnight. Maybe you should see someone. A therapist. A psychiatrist. About your anxiety, I mean. This isn't healthy."

"I don't know. I'll think about it."

Craig rose and gathered a couple of things from the kitchen counter.

"Where are you going?"

"Just to Zug. Not far."

Craig went into the spare bedroom where there were two clothes racks on wheels. The first one had women's dresses and blouses, and the one behind had his things. Rosario followed him. Craig rolled Rosaria's clothes out of the way and took a shirt off his rack. He walked over to a dresser and took out underwear and socks and put them and his shirt in a carryall.

"Why are you packing? You said you'd be back this evening."

"I may have to stay over if I don't get all the data I need tonight."

"What kind of data?"

"A financial company in Zug is allowing me to go over their accounts for a report I'm writing. My boss said the project was urgent."

"I'll wait up for you."

Craig crossed the room to where Rosaria was standing and kissed her on the cheek.

"Don't bother. Take care of yourself and get some sleep."

Craig left the apartment via the elevator. Upon exiting on the ground floor, he listened up the stairwell, then proceeded downstairs to the basement. He picked the lock of his neighbor's washer/dryer cage where he hid his equipment and entered it. Stretching his lengthy frame on his tiptoes, he brought down a bag from a concealed nook above the washer and opened it. His safecracking tools were all there, so he put them into his carryall. Then he checked the nook again and pulled down a gun with a shoulder holster. He gazed at it, passing it from one hand to the other. Then he replaced it in its hiding spot.

"Yes, I see him," Misha said into his phone from an alley across from Craig's apartment block. Then he hung up.

Craig walked out his front door, pulled his hood over his head, and turned right. The rain was coming down in a steady beat, heavy but now without a wind. He caught a trolley in the next street over and rode it to central Zurich. He exited the tram and ran into the entrance of a small hotel.

Misha parked his car in a spot where he could see the hotel entrance and waited.

In his room, Craig took out his bag and examined his tools: small and large picks and some electronic equipment.

They were all arrayed in a leather waist band. He replaced them, set his phone alarm, and lay down to sleep.

At midnight, Craig got up and left the hotel, wearing his tools under his slicker. He walked along Limmatquai, a street that runs along the Limmat, the river that flows out of Lake Zurich. His carryall was slung over his shoulder. The street was empty, and the rain was a deluge. Wind whooshed sheets of water across the street, creating a deafening sound as it hit the road and walls of nearby buildings. Craig looked over to the river and saw that it was overflowing its banks and flooding into the street.

Misha left his car and followed Craig to the bank. Then he calculated the route Craig would need to walk home. The trams had stopped running hours earlier.

Craig approached the front door of the Limmatquai Private Bank, took a tool from his waistband, and quickly dealt with the lock on the door. After entering, he pulled an electronic gadget from his belt, ran to the alarm next to the entrance, and disarmed it. Then he secured the front door behind him and crossed the lobby to a door with metal bars. He unlocked it and descended the stairs to a room with a large circular vault with two dials.

Craig rubbed his hands together to warm them. His fingers and acute sense of touch were all he needed to open safes. Craig placed his left hand on the door, his brow furrowed, and used his right hand to spin the dial. Assuming it was a three-digit combination, he spun the dial counterclockwise to clear the combination. While moving the dial back and forth, sometimes quickly, sometimes slowly, he found the combination and felt a satisfying click. Breathing a deep sigh, he glanced down at his feet and saw that he was standing in a puddle of rising water. He whipped his head around and looked at the staircase; a burbling stream of water descended them.

Craig repeated the steps he had taken with the first one, but when he expected a click, there was nothing. Glancing down, he saw the water was an inch deep, about two inches below the bottom edge of the vault door. Sweat poured down from his armpits. He paused, tapping his finger on the safe door, then tried again after spinning the lock. Turning the dial back and forth, he pursed his lips and shut his eyes tight. He opened his eyes and tried to open the door. It didn't budge.

The water was rising.

Then an old trick occurred to him, and he reversed the direction of the sequence of turns—clockwise first, then counterclockwise. The lower lock had a four-digit combination which you spun clockwise first, unlike the upper three-digit lock.

He opened the vault.

Craig draped his dripping wet coat on the spokes of the safe handle and pushed the door wide open. He pulled his shirt and undershirt from his bag, which was still slung over his shoulder, and threw them inside the safe area. After stepping into the room, he dried his shoes and pants. The chamber was full of safe deposit boxes on all four sides, with a table in the middle. *What was that smell? Oh, yeah: money.* With negative interest rates, the Swiss hoarded cash.

He hurried to the first box on his list and unlocked it with a pick. Inside, he found only jewelry and cash. Closing and replacing it, he moved on to the second box and opened that one. Inside were a set of six passports, and stacks of one thousand Swiss franc notes, worth about a thousand dollars. Each. Craig stared at the bills. He touched the top note on each stack, wondering if the owner would miss a strap, a mere $100,000 or so.

Who am I kidding? The Swiss count everything; they'd miss a centime.

And don't be crazy. You have a good job, a beautiful girlfriend, and a nice apartment—it beats the hell out of a jail cell! You've got to stay straight.

Craig rushed to the safe door and checked the water level, shuddering as he saw it was an inch from flowing over. He scrambled to the third box, trying to hold back his panic. He opened it, finding the Russians' plans for the arms shipment. After spreading the documents out on the table in the order they came from the box, he began photographing them with his phone. Halfway through, he checked the water level again—a half inch remaining. Craig wiped the moisture from his forehead and rubbed it off on his shirt. The last document was stapled with several pages. He snapped the papers while turning them, photographing page after page. Then he refilled the box and replaced it in the wall. Grabbing his clothes and bag, he stepped through the vault opening, being careful not to splash any water into the interior. He closed the door and twirled the dials just before the water could enter, leaving them in the exact placement that he had found them.

Gasping for air, Craig wiped more sweat from his brow and let out a low moan as he leaned against the safe door. He put on his coat and sloshed through the water, up the stairs, locking the door with bars behind him. Wading to the alarm, he rearmed it. After leaving the building, he checked that the front door was locked, then walked into the avalanche of water.

Craig headed toward his apartment on a hill on the west side of Zurich. He crossed the historic Münster bridge. On the other side, just beyond Fraumünster church, the water in Münsterhof plaza was about a foot deep. Running along the side of the cathedral to avoid the rain, he headed toward the overhang of the building in the middle of the square.

Misha, who had been hiding behind one of the pillars of the structure, jumped in front of Craig. "Hold it!"

Misha reached inside his coat to pull out his gun. Still running, Craig flicked off his bag, throwing it at Misha's arm. Then he leapt forward and grabbed Misha's hand, twisting it, until the gun dropped. Misha moved to pick it up, but it had disappeared into the water. Craig pushed him and struck his face, but to little effect. Misha, a much bigger man, launched himself at Craig, tackled him, knocking him into the water. Misha put his hands around Craig's throat and pushed his head under the water. Craig used his left elbow to elevate himself out of the water, gulped some air, and tried to gouge Misha's eyes with his right thumb, but Misha turned his head away and shoved Craig below the lake that occupied the square. Craig raised his head a second time, gasping, and tried to break Misha's hold on his throat by pushing outward with his arms, but to no avail. Misha forced Craig's head under the water again and Craig's struggling weakened. Then Craig's hand emerged from the water with one of his longer lock picks. Craig thrust it into Misha's neck, once, twice, and then a third time. Blood spurted out of Misha's throat and his movements slowed. His grip on Craig loosened. Craig shoved Misha off, panting heavily.

"And that one's for Audrey!" Craig said, stabbing Misha one last time in the jugular. Craig recognized Misha from the CIA files on Russian agents. He was one of Russia's more notorious assassins; fake suicides were his modus operandi.

Craig staggered to his feet. Misha sank into the water, his pale face illuminated by the streetlamps, blood swirling from his wound. His shocked eyes were still open.

Craig grabbed the big man by his lapels and, struggling, dragged him over to the elevated walkway under the building's overhang. He checked all the pockets, grabbing Misha's phone and wallet, for any information they might contain. Then he took his watch, even though it was a Rolex knockoff, to make it look like a mugging. Craig felt a pang of remorse when he tried taking off his wedding ring. It was stuck fast to his finger; he'd have to leave it. Then he vomited into the plaza's lake.

It was his first kill.

Craig rifled through Misha's wallet—over five hundred in Swiss francs. He left the cash; seeing it made him feel empty.

He awakened the phone and put it to Misha's face to unlock it. Then he reset its password so it would be easy to open again. Before shutting it down, he checked Misha's recent calls and messages. What he found gave him a headache and made him throw up again.

Recovering, Craig picked up his bag, stepped over Misha, slogged across Zurich, and climbed the street to his apartment. Upon arrival, he unlocked the front door using his key. As usual, the lights came on automatically.

Craig cocked his ear, listening. Hearing nothing, he descended to the basement, dripping water behind him. He picked his neighbor's lock, entered, and stretched to find his gun. Finding it, he returned his tools to the nook. He then put his satchel and his coat in his own cage.

Gun in hand, Craig climbed the stairs, pausing to listen at each landing. When he reached his apartment, he turned the key in the lock so as not to make a noise, then opened the door from a crouching position. The place was quiet; all the lights were out. He stepped into the flat, checking the bedroom first. Rosaria was sleeping in their bed. Her heavy breathing indicated she might be dreaming. He walked over to her.

"Craig. Your home!" Rosaria said, sitting bolt upright, her voice choking. It was all she got out. Craig whacked her on the side of the head with his gun.

"You betrayed me!" Craig shouted at her limp body.

Who am I? I kill a man, then I hit a woman with a gun. I've never done anything like that before. I hate this business!

Sighing, Craig wiped the blood from Rosaria's head wound and checked her breathing and pulse. She'd live. Then Craig cut off the cord from his vacuum cleaner and tied her up, securing her to the bed, so she couldn't make an escape or fall off. Then he taped her mouth with duct tape. No one would be able to help him until morning, and he didn't want to wake up with a knife in his back. He was bone tired and knew he wouldn't make it through the night without nodding off.

He phoned Marshall and apprised him of the night's events. Marshall castigated him for trusting Rosaria and lying to him about where she was living. Then he insisted Craig immediately send the arms shipment documents to him.

He only congratulated Craig after he had received and reviewed them.

Craig surveyed his apartment. Rosaria's packed bags were near the door. She had searched the apartment. The furniture was overturned, his clothes strewn everywhere. On Rosaria's rack there was one pathetic rejected dress. Returning to the living room, Craig smiled as he saw Pud appear from underneath the overturned couch. Pud meowed, and Craig stooped to pick her up.

"It's OK. Everything is alright," Craig said, stroking Pud's head. "Even you saw that coming, but I didn't, eh, Pud?"

Craig put the cat on the counter. After taking a tin of cat food from a cabinet, he fed Pud, who wolfed down her food. Then he retrieved a bottle of red wine from a rack on the counter, uncorked it, and poured himself a glass. Crossing the living room to the French windows, he opened them, and stepped onto the balcony, glass in hand.

The rain had stopped, and the moon was peeking out from the clouds. Craig lifted his glass, toasted the moon, and took a sip.

TWO DEATHS IN VENICE

The pizza place off the Campo San Polo in Venice didn't look like much, but it was pouring down rain, and Kevin was starving. After walking by it twice to find a better place nearby, he decided this was his best bet. As he entered and oriented himself, the aroma of cheap pizza assaulted his nose. The pizzeria's tourist-trap décor consisted of intense florescent lighting, linoleum floors, and cafeteria-style tables arranged in rows for communal eating. At least the tables had chairs, not benches. Finding a seat would be easy; except for one lone diner sitting in a corner, the place was empty.

Kevin's stomach sank. He was looking forward to a relaxing weekend in Venice. He could afford dinner at a fine restaurant but was too tired and wet to look for one. It had been a long day, and now all he could expect was a mediocre meal with a glass of rough wine. He'd flown in early Friday morning from London to be the last speaker at an insurance conference. The speech was successful; the other participants had many questions about his talk on Solvency II regulations and the insurance industry. It was October 2012, and Kevin made the tedious and opaque topic mildly amusing, much to the appreciation of the audience.

At this place, you needed to order a pizza—all they had—and your beverage at the counter, pay, and then find a seat; they would bring the food to you. The menu had a wide variety of pizzas and two types of wine: *rosso e bianco*. Kevin ordered a sausage pizza and a glass of red wine. The wine was given to him immediately after he paid, so Kevin turned to find a seat, drink in hand.

I'm sure they'll be able to find me in this crowd, Kevin thought as he settled into an empty table facing the windows and entry door. Sometimes waiters had difficulty finding him in a throng. He was slim, above-average height, middle-aged, with thinning brown hair and a weak chin. Nondescript in every way.

The pizza came promptly, and Kevin was nearly finished eating when another customer entered. The new person was of medium height and build, wearing a soaking wet gray jacket, black pants, and a white shirt. He wore a fedora pulled tight over his face and tilted toward Kevin when he entered. He walked briskly to the person seated alone in the corner behind Kevin.

Bang!

The gunfire was deafening in the small confines of the pizzeria. Kevin grabbed his left ear and turned toward the noise. The gunman shielded his face from Kevin by shifting his hat to the right side of his face and ran to the door, leaving his victim's slumped and bloody body behind him. Kevin followed his movement with his head, his body rigid.

When the man opened the door, a gust of wind blew his hat off. He turned to pick it up, and his eyes locked onto Kevin's, who continued to stare at him, petrified.

The man picked up his hat and put it on his head while holding the door open with his back foot. He raised his gun, pointing it at Kevin, who was still frozen. Then he pulled the trigger. Nothing. He tried again. No response. The gun had jammed.

Kevin couldn't move. He felt like he was watching a black-and-white film noir; Humphrey Bogart would enter at any moment. *Is this how it ends? Where's Bogart?*

Then, hearing a police boat siren from the nearby canal, the killer turned and fled through the open door.

Kevin's immediate thought was, *I hope I didn't pee myself.* He was relieved to feel his crotch was dry. His second thought was, *I need a drink.* He put the last bite of pizza in his mouth and headed for the counter.

"I'll have a half carafe of red, thank you," he said to the person lying flat on the floor behind the counter. The server lifted himself, staring at Kevin like he was crazy. But business was business, and he recovered, filled a carafe with wine, and took Kevin's payment which included a generous tip.

Kevin sat down again in his seat, the empty pizza tray in front of him. He looked over at the lifeless form in the corner. The man had fallen to the floor, and his head was still oozing blood. A large puddle of red covered the linoleum in front of his face, his unseeing eyes still wide open. Kevin looked away. *No need to see that again,* he thought, downing a large glass of wine. *Maybe I should get out of here before the police arrive? No, that wouldn't be right.*

The police arrived a few minutes later. No sirens announced their arrival; whatever the gunman had heard earlier was unrelated to the pizzeria event. A lucky break for Kevin.

The two *carabinieri* rushed in the front door. One went to the dead body, the other approached Kevin. Their uniforms were black with a red stripe theme: stripes on their pants, the belt sash across their chests, and on their epaulets. Their hats had a red rim and yellowish plumage at the front.

Recognizing Kevin as American, the officer spoke to him in English. This irked Kevin. *Why is it so obvious I'm American? I'm wearing a Canali suit.*

"I'm Officer Vanzetti, and I need to ask you some questions," the officer said to Kevin.

"Like as in, Sacco and Vanzetti?" Kevin asked.

"No relation," he replied. The officer had clearly heard of the infamous anarchists, executed for crimes they probably didn't commit, but he had no interest in being associated with them. Meanwhile, his partner was speaking on his phone while examining the body, probably requesting the forensics people and an ambulance. The bright lights made Kevin feel like he was in one of those movies where the police grill you while shining a spotlight in your eyes. The officer then asked Kevin for his passport, which Kevin always carried with him when traveling.

"OK. I'm ready," Kevin said, downing the last of his wine.

"Mr. Lewis, did you see who shot the man at the corner table?" Officer Vanzetti asked.

This is a fucking mess! I'm a witness to a murder in a foreign country, and I'm just here for the weekend. Will this investigation delay my return to work?

"Please answer the question," Vanzetti said.

"Yes. I did," Kevin said. It was the right thing to do. He hoped it wouldn't be too complicated. People shouldn't be allowed to walk into pizza joints and blow someone away. Also, the killer had ruined his dinner, such as it was. Unforgiveable.

"Did you get a good look at him?"

"Yes."

"Could you identify him if you saw his photo?"

"Probably."

"OK. We're going to the police station, and we'll ask you to identify the shooter from a series of photographs." Kevin noted the officer had still not returned his passport.

"OK. Can I use the restroom first?"

"Yes. I'll wait outside the door."

Kevin entered the Men's Room and went into a stall. Having finished, he went to wash his hands. He looked at the window and wondered if he could get out of it to escape. *Bad idea. Then I'd be the hunted.*

Kevin accompanied Vanzetti to the Cai Duohua police station, three minutes from the plaza. They passed by the San Polo church that had works by Tiepolo and Tintoretto. Kevin made a mental note to visit it, hopefully, the next day. The rain had eased, so they didn't need their umbrellas.

Kevin imagined he would be looking through large books of photos, but of course, everything was digital. Vanzetti placed him in front of a computer terminal, spoke to a colleague, and faces began appearing on the screen at five-second intervals.

After fifteen minutes had passed, and one-hundred eighty photos, Kevin was feeling drowsy. His eyelids were heavy; sitting down had allowed his body to unwind from the tension of the shooting and the gun that fortuitously refused to discharge a bullet at him. Also, the wine was having the desired effect. Then, finally, a photo of the perpetrator appeared on the screen.

"Wait!" Kevin said. "That looks like him."

"Are you sure?" Vanzetti said.

"Yes. That's him, alright," Kevin said. "I thought we'd never find him."

Vanzetti spoke to his colleague, and a mix of photos of the murderer and similar-looking suspects appeared, but Kevin repeatedly identified the same man.

"You've done well," Vanzetti said. "But now I'll need to keep your passport. We're asking you to stay in Venice for a few days, so we can round this man up and put him in a lineup for you to identify again. It appears to be a killing by a rival Latin American gang member, probably over a woman."

Kevin reluctantly let them keep his passport. He needed it to return to London and his insurance company job. *Shit. Why is this so problematic? Ah, well, there are worse cities in the world to be held hostage.*

At his hotel, Kevin emailed his boss, apprising him of the situation. He would not cancel his flight for now. Venice isn't a large town, and it's densely populated. If the guy was still on the island, they should be able to find him quickly. Then he poured himself two scotches from the minibar, drank them, and went to bed.

The next day, Kevin proceeded with his original plan: visit museums, churches, and other tourist attractions and eat fabulous food. *No more pizza!*

He started at the church they had walked by the previous evening since it was close to his hotel. The church and its paintings were magnificent. Unfortunately, he wasn't an expert on Italian Renaissance art; he guessed Tiepolo's paintings were the lighter colored ones compared to Tintoretto's, which always seemed dark, foreboding, and full of dead people.

October typically has a lot of rain, and this month was no different. One advantage to this weekend was that there were few tourists since no cruise ships were visiting. The low volume of people and lack of vehicles created a still, serene atmosphere. The air was fresh with the scent of the recent rain. Kevin's greatest joys in the city included wandering through the maze of alleys, crossing canals via small bridges, and discovering a specialty olive store or a quaint restaurant. There were many plain white houses and pastel ones, ranging in color from yellow to reddish-orange. Even without the sun, they provided a pleasant glow to his stroll. Sadly, many structures needed repairs, but they still looked magnificent. The architecture was exquisitely detailed, with many buildings constructed during the Renaissance when wealthy families vied to have the most beautiful fronts to their Palazzos. Many buildings had intricate windows and features; some had columns and sculptures.

From the Campo San Polo, he made his way to the *Gallerie dell'Accademia*. As he walked across the plaza in front of the building, it began to drizzle again. He was glad to get inside but shocked to see how few people were visiting; there were more guards than tourists. It was eerie wandering alone through the high-ceiling galleries and viewing the enormous paintings. There was little light, and the silence was tangible with minimal other guests. Though unnerving—Kevin worried the gunman would appear from around a corner at any moment—it was also strangely soothing. The coolness of the fall air penetrated all corners of the museum, creating a faint haze in the venue.

It was a short walk to the Peggy Guggenheim Collection from the *Gallerie*. The permanent collection in that museum was interesting, but the special exhibit of the Fauvism school was exhilarating. Kevin recognized many of the painter's names but had never heard of the Fauvism movement. André Derain and Maurice de Vlaminck were well-represented, new artists to Kevin, but so were Matisse and Braque. The colors on the canvases were bright and immediate, a delightful slap in the face. Kevin meandered through all the rooms, lingering longest in the largest Fauvism room.

Back outside in the autumn breeze, Kevin headed to his hotel. He crossed the *Ponte dell'Accademia* but spotted the hitman on the other side! Worse, the killer saw him. Kevin reached for his cell to call the police, but it was dead; he'd been using it all day to navigate and take photos. The murderer began weaving through a small group of people toward Kevin, who looked around for an escape route. Retreating across the bridge wouldn't work; there was nowhere to hide. Dashing into an alleyway would be like walking into your own mausoleum. No police were in sight. Creating a commotion might backfire.

Then, he saw a gondola in the canal with two people disembarking. He jumped aboard, thrust a hundred euro note into the gondolier's hand, and shouted "*Presto!*" while pointing to the far side of the Grand Canal. The gondolier shook his head in disgust at Kevin's rudeness but pushed off rapidly after pocketing the money. Kevin saw his nemesis grinding his teeth and glaring at him from the canal's edge as they pulled away. The gondolier took Kevin to a transport terminal on the opposite side of the channel, where Kevin hopped on the next ferry, which luckily was going toward his hotel.

After landing, Kevin dove into the warren of alleyways near his hotel. Spotting a clothing store, he lunged inside to find an outfit less noticeable than his suit. He picked out a shirt, a jacket, and a hat, putting them on and placing his suit coat and dress shirt into a bag.

Why didn't I do this earlier? Could I make myself any more conspicuous in my suit?

He was disoriented and lost his way in the alleys. At one point, he stumbled upon a street fair in a small piazza where the merchants had laid out their wares on blankets. Something caught his eye; it was a switchblade. He tried the mechanism, and the blade came out swiftly. It seemed cheap and flimsy, but, on an impulse, he bought it, stuffing it into his back pocket.

At the hotel, he called the police to tell them he saw the assassin, so they would know the killer was still in the city. For dinner, the hotel manager recommended a neighborhood hole-in-the-wall frequented by locals, not tourists. Kevin enjoyed an excellent meal of *linguine alle vongole*, rabbit stew, and salad at the *trattoria*. He had a generous glass of Soave with the linguine and two Refoscos with the meat dish.

Feeling refreshed and satiated, he left the restaurant and headed toward his hotel. The route included many twists and turns down dark passageways. Turning around one corner, he bumped into a medium-height man wearing a hat who looked up at him, startled. It was the murderer from the pizzeria! *Twice in one day! How bad is my luck?*

The man reached in his jacket and drew out a gun, which Kevin immediately grabbed with his left hand, lifting it upwards. But the killer held on tight, thrusting his free hand at Kevin's throat. Kevin reached for the knife in his back pocket and drew it out, pressing the button to release the blade.

Nothing happened.

The man shifted his hand from Kevin's neck to his wrist. Kevin tried the control again, but still no stiletto.

This switchblade is as bad as this guy's gun!

They continued to struggle, with no one gaining any ground. They both held the gun firmly, and the killer tried to squeeze Kevin's wrist so hard that he would drop the knife.

It was a stalemate, but Kevin realized he had an advantage in height. He lifted his right arm and twisted it into the shorter man's thumb, releasing his armed hand. Kevin pressed the button a final time and plunged the switchblade at the man's neck, hoping to rip a hole in his trachea with the metal stub. The man seized his hand again and pulled it away from his neck. Kevin glanced at his knife but still couldn't see the blade on it.

Being larger, Kevin, keeping his eye on the gun, pushed the man toward the alley wall, thinking he could bang his hand against it. But, as he slowly edged the guy closer to the wall, the killer's grip on the gun weakened, and his knees buckled.

Kevin looked into his eyes. They were glazing over, and his mouth had gone slack. It was then that Kevin saw the blood spurting from the man's neck and the broken blade of his knife protruding from his jugular.

The man slumped and fell lifeless to the ground, leaving Kevin holding the gun.

Kevin stared at the dead body. No one was nearby. No one had heard them struggling. In his panic, Kevin had forgotten to call for help. He listened. Nothing. He wiped his prints off the gun and put it back in the man's hand. Then he threw the switchblade handle into a nearby canal. His jacket was covered in blood; he removed it and wadded it up to hide the stains. Taking a tissue from his pocket, he dabbed blood on it from his shirt, folding it carefully to leave a bloodless area. He certainly didn't want any germs from the dead man. Then he threw back his head, put the clean part of the handkerchief to his nose, and walked away.

Out of the labyrinth of alleys, he saw a few people. He pointed to his nose with his free hand and said, "Nosebleed." They probably didn't speak English, but he couldn't stop himself. He said the same thing to the manager when he reached the hotel, hand still clutching the tissue to his nose.

The following morning, Kevin rose early, jammed the bloody shirt, jacket, and his recently acquired hat into a plastic laundry bag, and walked out of the hotel. He went several blocks and found another row of dumpsters, where he carefully disposed of the sack. Kevin returned to the hotel, served himself an espresso, and sat in the breakfast area. He was just finishing his second *cornetto* when the two police officers arrived.

"Mr. Lewis, we'd like you to come with us," Vanzetti said. "We think we have found the suspect." Meanwhile, the other officer chatted with the manager.

"Sure. Just let me grab my coat from my room." He returned downstairs in his dark-gray Canali suit, tieless.

They strode out of the hotel but arrived at the morgue instead of the police station. They checked in at the front desk, and the attendant led them down a long hallway to a cold room. He then opened one of the chamber drawers, rolled out a corpse, and lifted the sheet off the body.

"Is this the man you saw in the pizzeria?" Vanzetti asked.

"Yes," Kevin replied. "That's him."

"OK. We need to return to the police station to complete some forms."

At the station, Vanzetti took Kevin to an interrogation room with a single table, two chairs, and a one-way mirror.

"Don't worry," Vanzetti said. "We're short on rooms; this is a quiet place to wait."

About a half-hour later, Vanzetti entered the room and sat opposite Kevin. "We understand you returned to the hotel at about ten p.m. last night."

"That sounds right."

"The manager said you had blood on your shirt when you arrived."

"Yes. After I left the restaurant, I got a nosebleed, and some of it got on a cheap shirt I bought yesterday."

"What happened to the shirt? The hotel staff couldn't find it in your room."

"I took it out this morning and threw it away. I didn't want the cleaning staff to have to deal with it. It was pretty ugly."

"Do you remember where you discarded it?"

"I think I could find the place. Why? What's the problem?"

"We don't believe you had anything to do with the suspect's death, but we need to eliminate any loose ends in the case. Your return to the hotel coincides with the deceased's time of death."

"OK. Shall we look for the trash can?" Kevin did not know what else to do. Would he have to confess to this killing?

They headed toward the hotel, and with a heavy heart, Kevin pointed to the bin where he recalled leaving the shirt. It didn't make sense to finger the wrong trash container; if they didn't find the shirt, they would still become suspicious of him.

The junior officer walked up to the dumpster and lifted its lid, poking his head inside.

Kevin watched him, his stomach tight, sweat pouring down from his armpits. *Am I going to be arrested? This would put a dent in my career.*

The officer continued to peer into the trash bin as if reflecting on something. *What does he see?*

He turned toward Kevin and Vanzetti and said, "It's empty."

Vanzetti made a call and confirmed that the trash had been put on a barge that morning. It was now on its way to its final resting spot along with several other ships, all full of garbage.

At the police station, Kevin was again shut into the interrogation room while Vanzetti and his partner discussed the case in the corridor.

"What do you think?" Vanzetti asked.

"Mr. Lewis doesn't look like a killer. It's hard to imagine this humdrum insurance executive stabbing anyone."

"I agree. He doesn't seem the type nor competent enough to knife someone in the throat. Also, what we have right now are two dead gang members. I think we can leave this second killing unsolved. The city of Venice is better off without these hoodlums."

They returned to the room where Kevin was seated and handed him his passport.

"Sign here, and you're free to go."

Kevin signed and walked back to his hotel. He packed his suitcase, took the water bus to the airport, and caught his flight back to London. He flew business class and partook generously of the wine served by the flight attendants.

DEATH BENEFITS

Damian stood across from his boss's desk, dressed—as usual—in a light gray suit, white shirt, and pencil-thin black tie. He was short but muscled. A former cop, he worked out regularly at the gym. He still wore his hair in a crew cut. Some habits die hard.

"I just don't buy it," Clay Brewer said. "It's too convenient for this company to get a million-dollar insurance payout now."

"I have a copy of the suicide note," Damian said, passing the letter to his boss. "It's pretty clear."

> *I can't go on. I shouldn't have taken the money from Cross Water Systems. I see nothing in my future. I'm sorry.*
> *Abby*

"Who types a suicide note?" Clay said. "No one! What female shoots herself in the head? None!"

"Her sister verified the signature, and there have been other cases of typed suicide letters."

"I never should have signed off on these company life insurance policies. Cross had too many financial problems."

"The lady's dead."

"I know, and I'm sorry about that," Clay said. "But if it's fraud, then we don't have to pay the claim."

"Are you suggesting that someone at Cross Water Systems killed Ms. Clarke to collect this insurance?"

"The timing is a little too handy for my taste. The company's barely surviving, and this will bail them out. Your job is to find out what the hell really happened. I'll stall on the claim."

"Yes, sir. I'm on it."

Damian reviewed the facts of the case. Abby Clarke was found dead in her living room, a bullet wound in her right temple, a gun at her feet with her fingerprints on it. Abby's sister, Angela Neal, found the body and the suicide note. Angela, a struggling single mom, became concerned after being unable to reach Abby. Just before her death, Abby was accused of embezzling $40,000 from Cross Water Systems. Daphne Cross, the CEO of CWS, had provided evidence of this to the police. Abby was single and lived alone, never having married.

Abby was the Chief Financial Officer for CWS, a firm dealing in the installation of water purification systems. The third principal at CWS was Ward Bennett, Chief Sales Officer. Daphne had taken out key person insurance on Abby and Ward. If either person died, the company would be paid the death benefit of one million dollars. As the owner, Daphne had not insured herself; death bestows a certain amount of indifference to worldly things. Despite the grandiose titles for the executives, CWS was a small company with thirteen employees and revenue of two million in a good year. However, there hadn't been many good years recently, and the company was on the brink of bankruptcy. The one million payout would be enough to clear the firm's debts, so it could continue to operate.

There was nowhere to start except at the beginning: Abby's sister.

Angela opened the door to her modest South Philadelphia row house after Damian knocked on it. He introduced himself and said, "If I may, I'd like to ask you a few questions about your sister, Abby."

"The police closed the case, ruling it a suicide." Angela started to close the door.

"I know," Damian said, putting his foot in the door opening. "Raxalan examines every claim over one million as a part of our responsibility to our shareholders. Cross Water System's life insurance policy meets the criteria."

"Abby had life insurance?" Angela asked, a tremor in her voice, letting the door swing open. CWS wasn't required to tell relatives about the policy; the company only needed the employee's permission. So Damian wasn't surprised that Angela hadn't heard of the coverage.

"It's complicated. Let me in and I'll explain it."

"Sure. I'm sorry. Please come in and make yourself comfortable. Can I get you coffee or water?"

"A coffee would be great. Thanks." Damian knew Angela needed time to process this new information, and he could always use a coffee.

He surveyed his surroundings. Toys were strewn about randomly; a couch pillow was on the floor; the TV was an ancient model, like something from a museum. Angela was about forty years old, tall, hefty, with sandy brown hair, brown eyes, and disheveled clothes. She had seen better days, but those were long gone.

Angela brought two coffees into the living room and sat on a sofa across from Damian, her body rigid. After expressing his sympathy for her loss, Damian explained the insurance policy. "It's what's called Company Owned Life Insurance. CWS is the owner and beneficiary of the policy. Unfortunately, there is nothing for the family of the deceased."

"Oh," Angela said, her face drooping as she let out a deep sigh.

Damian delicately probed Angela's reaction to her sister's death.

"It was so sudden, so unexpected. I would never have thought Abby would commit suicide. Nor did I ever think she could take money from Cross. Abby was the most honest person I knew," Angela said, her eyes welling up with tears. Damian offered her his handkerchief, but she shook her head and wiped her eyes with her hand.

"Were the two of you close?"

"Yes, very, but something happened over the past year. Abby became distant, and we saw a lot less of each other. I suspect she was seeing someone, but whenever I asked, she turned away, but always with a wistful smile," Angela said, shaking her head.

"So, if there was a boyfriend, you never met him?" Damian asked, trying not to show too much interest.

"No. But I sensed she was in a relationship. I don't know why."

"I know this is painful for you, and you've been over it perhaps several times with the police, but could you tell me about the day you found your sister?"

"Oh, Mr. Webb," Angela said, "why are you here?"

Damian again explained his fiduciary duty to investigate the claim.

"OK," Angela said, her shoulders slumping, "I'll do my best, but it's hard."

"I understand. Take as long as you like."

"Well, my kids get home soon, so I must be quick."

"Shall we start?"

"I had phoned my sister a few times in the three days before visiting her home. But I only got voice mail. I was worried because normally, she phones me right back. So, I went to her house when the kids were at school. I have a key, just as she has...had a key to my place. As soon as I opened the door, I knew something was wrong; it stank. She was slumped in her favorite chair, lifeless."

Angela broke down and sobbed but continued, "She was dead. Her gun was on the floor. I called the police."

"The door was locked when you entered?"

"Yes, it locks when you close it behind you."

"There were no signs of a struggle or anything out of place?"

"No, it was tidy as always. I found the note on her desk in front of the computer."

"The suicide note?"

"I verified to the police the signature was hers. I gave them examples from cards she sent me, and they decided it was the same. It seemed odd that she typed the note, but that was Abby; she was always meticulous. She bought the gun after there was an attempted burglary in her neighborhood. It was meant to protect her, not kill her," Angela said, her voice choking.

"Would you mind if I went to her house and looked around?" Again, Damian was subdued, feigning a lack of curiosity.

"What do you expect to find? It's still a mess; I didn't clean up the blood. I just haven't had the energy."

"Our investigations are thorough. Then, we put all the information into a report. It's just procedure."

"I suppose. Here are the keys," she said, retrieving them from a side cupboard next to the TV, her steps weary with defeat.

"Thank you for your time, Ms. Neal. Again, please accept my condolences."

Damian took the keys and returned to his car, parked a block away on the narrow street. He recorded a brief report on his boss's voice mail, indicating he may be onto something, and that Clay should continue to delay the claim payment.

It was a twenty-minute drive to Abby's house in Society Hill, but a world away from Angela's house in South Philly. Being single had its financial advantages. Damian knew this from his personal experience; he was an inveterate bachelor. He hoped Angela's former husband paid child support and alimony; she clearly needed it.

The front door opened into the living room, a typical row house layout. Someone had opened a couple of windows, but the place still smelled. Damian immediately saw the chair, covered in blood, where Abby had died. The desk was opposite;

Abby must have watched videos on her computer screen since there was no TV in the room. Damian sat at the desk and turned on the computer. There was no password protection, so he searched Abby's email but found nothing interesting. Then, he decided to look into the Trash folder.

A deleted email revealed that someone was scheduled to visit Abby, at home, on the day of her death. He printed it out.

He checked her bank account and financial accounts; all the passwords were auto-filled. The police had found she had the $40,000 in an account at a local bank. However, the only bank on this machine was a national one, and it only had enough for her monthly needs.

However, her IRA had over $500,000 in it. Why would she steal $40,000? It didn't make any sense. He also found her will on file and printed it; everything, including her house, was to go to her sister. It warmed his heart to read that.

Damian began to search the house methodically. Nothing in the living room, not even behind the accounting manuals on the bookcase; nothing in the kitchen nor any of the cabinets; nothing in the spare bedroom, but in the main bedroom, he discovered something strange. One of the bedside tables had a much shallower drawer than its matching one on the other side. After feeling around, he located a trick latch that popped out a hidden compartment beneath the drawer. It contained a diary. The early entries were about Abby's dreams and aspirations, the occasional flirtation, and fun days with Angela and her kids. However, the accounts from the past year were almost exclusively about her boyfriend. They detailed how sweet he was to her, how he helped her with her work, bought her flowers and expensive bottles of wine, and how much she loved him. But she couldn't tell anyone about their relationship.

She had been dating Ward Bennett.

The following morning, Damian asked for an urgent meeting with Clay.

"I need to talk to our clients at Cross Water Systems," Damian said, "and it's going to be tricky." He filled in Clay on what he had discovered.

"You have my permission," Clay replied. "Smoke 'em out!"

Where does he get that talk? Damian thought. *We're a frigging insurance company.*

Back at his desk, he arranged a meeting with Ward and Daphne in their offices. They were eager to settle the whole matter so CSW could receive its insurance payment but were having a busy day and could only see him in the evening.

Daphne welcomed Damian from behind her desk and motioned for him to sit opposite her. Ward was seated to her right. Neither rose to greet him. The room was spartan, with one chair in front of Daphne's desk, two large filing cabinets, and a small conference table with chairs to Daphne's left. Ward was tall, with dyed blond hair, blue eyes, a square jaw, and broad shoulders. A real lady-killer. Daphne was medium height, with carefully coifed light brown hair, precise makeup, and stylish clothes. Though pleasing to the eye, she exuded the hard-edged confidence of a CEO. You wouldn't want to mess with her.

After he was seated, Daphne asked when they could expect their payment. He explained that he needed to complete a claim report before Raxalan could release the death benefit.

"How can we help you?" Daphne asked.

"We need to tie up loose ends about Ms. Clarke's death," Damian said.

"Suicide," Daphne corrected.

"Yes, we're still trying to understand that," Damian said. "Did either of you know Abby well? Did you ever socialize with her, for example? Get to know her as a person?"

"I didn't," Daphne said. "We were never on social terms. We'd chat at the Christmas party and such, but that was about it."

Ward squirmed in his chair, glanced nervously at Daphne, but said nothing. Daphne, focused on Damian, missed Ward's quick look at her.

"You, Ward?" Damian asked with all the innocence he could muster.

"We were just colleagues. I'd detail the sales to her; she'd invoice them."

"Abby died on a Saturday, and I'm sure you saw her at work on Friday," Damian said and paused; they both nodded. "But did either of you see her on the day of her death?"

"Where exactly are you going with this, Mr. Webb?" Daphne asked.

"We're trying to understand why Abby might have decided to commit suicide."

"Well, I didn't tell the police this because I didn't think it would help," Daphne said. "The poor woman is dead. But I visited her home to discuss our evidence about her embezzling the money from Cross Water Systems."

"How did she take it?"

"She was distraught and denied everything, but we have the evidence, and the police are investigating. We should be able to recover the money from her estate."

"So, you were the last person to see her alive?"

"Yes, apparently so. We didn't know why she wasn't at work the next Monday and Tuesday and heard about the tragedy from her sister, Angela Neal."

"Do you think it may have given her a reason to commit suicide?"

"I can't speculate on what was going through Abby's mind," Daphne said. "I was surprised she said she hadn't taken the money. Who else could have done it?"

"Would you mind if I reviewed the transactions that were suspect?" Damian asked.

"Whatever for?"

"I'd like to establish a motive for her death."

"Very well," Daphne said, sighing heavily. Shaking her head in disbelief, she retrieved a file from one of the cabinets and handed it to Damian.

"Thank you," Damian said. "Ward, I have interviewed someone who thought you were dating Ms. Clarke." Damian had always found the out-of-the-blue, unexpected questions received the most revealing responses.

After taking a deep breath and looking anxiously at Daphne, Ward said, "Who told you that?" This time, Daphne saw the look and her eyes widened and her nostrils flared.

"I have my sources."

Ward paused, then said, "Well, I guess it might as well all come out. I was dating Abby, but we were keeping it secret. It's not considered proper these days to have a girlfriend from the office, even if you are equal partners. And...I didn't want Daphne to know."

"Ward! I'm surprised by this," Daphne said. "Why didn't you tell me? We're a small team; such a relationship could have ruined us!"

"That's precisely why we didn't tell you. We were only going to let everyone know when we decided to get married."

"Get married!" Daphne said, electricity rippling through the room.

Daphne shook her head, smoothed her skirt, and said, "Mr. Webb, you seem to have become witness to the messy business life we have here at Cross Water Systems. I apologize; you shouldn't have to hear about our dirty laundry."

"Not a problem. I've witnessed much worse. You do realize that your fondness for Ward and a possible COLI payout provide you with a motive to murder Abby Clarke, don't you?"

"That's absurd. I would never kill anyone, and I can assure you that my interest in Mr. Bennett is now greatly diminished. However," she continued, "I think it is time you were leaving, Mr. Webb. And I still expect to receive our death benefit once you have finished your 'report.'"

After closing the door, Damian stopped to listen to the uproar from the office but didn't hear any confessions, just accusative screeches from Daphne and whining from Ward.

How am I going to pin this death on one of these two? Damian thought as he headed to his car.

The following Friday, Damian tailed Ward after he left the office. Instead of going to his home, Ward went straight to the local casino. Damian watched him enter from his car, waited an hour, then strode into the gambling hall.

It didn't take long to locate Ward; he was at a craps table, losing badly. Damian watched at a distance until Ward was out of money.

"Hello, Ward. Can I buy you a drink?" Ward's head jerked back in shock and surprise, but he recovered.

"What are you doing here?" Ward demanded.

"I sometimes like to gamble, but I've never seen you here. Do you come often?"

"I enjoy it. I come here sometimes to unwind. It's thrilling when I win, but not so fun when I lose. So, yes, I'll take a drink."

"Is craps your favorite game? I like blackjack, myself," Damian said once they were seated at a tall table near the bar. Damian had noted that the bartender greeted Ward by his first name when he ordered their drinks.

"Yes, it's my usual."

They bantered about gambling, the weather, the Phillies, and how people dressed when they came to casinos. Damian patiently waited for the double whiskey to kick in.

"So, it was you that was embezzling the funds from Cross?" After reviewing the file Daphne gave him, Damian matched the transactions with those mentioned in Abby's diary; Ward had helped Abby on all those invoices. He must have opened an account in Abby's name to use as a private piggy bank to feed his gambling habit.

Ward sobered abruptly, his head snapped up, and he looked Damian in the eye with a fierce rage.

"I imagine you had a few words about it before she died," Damian said. "She must have figured out you had fudged the books."

"Yes, I embezzled the funds, but I didn't kill her. I loved her!"

They spent another hour in heated conversation, but Damian couldn't get Ward to budge: he didn't do it, and he was sticking to that story.

Both of them had a motive to kill Abby, but how will I get enough evidence to get a confession?

The following day, Damian dropped by Angela's house to return the key to Abby's home. Fortunately, the kids were with their father that weekend. Nevertheless, the living room was in the same state as when he last saw it; toys covered the floor.

"Oh, Mr. Webb," Angela said, tidying her hair, "thanks for returning the key. Please excuse the mess. Let me get you some coffee."

"Sure. I can always use a cup of java."

"Do you always work alone?"

"Yes, and my office rarely knows where I am."

"How is your report coming along?"

"Nearly finished. But I do have one question."

"Sure, what can I do for you?"

"One of Abby's neighbors said they saw you entering Abby's home the night she died," Damian said, recalling the deleted email exchange between Abby and her sister.

"Is that in your report?"

"No, should it be?"

"I don't see why. That might be problematic for me."

"Oh?"

"Mr. Webb, I'm forgetting my manners; let me get you your coffee."

Angela returned from the kitchen, taking long strides, a large chef knife in her right hand. Damian stood to face her and dodged to the side when she went to stab him, grabbing her hand, pulling it downward, and flipping his back into her stomach. She began pummeling him in the kidneys with surprising strength.

"Abby was always the favorite child; she was the successful one; she had so much, and she never shared," Angela said through clenched teeth. "Now, I'll be damned if I'm going to let some gumshoe deprive me of my inheritance."

While holding her right hand with his left, he raised his right arm and popped her head with his elbow. Her movements slowed, but she continued hitting him in the back. He slammed her again. And again.

Damn, this lady is strong. Who would've thought a stay-at-home mom would be in such good shape?

Finally, after another blow to her head, Angela collapsed to the floor, unconscious.

Damian stood still, the knife now in his hand, gazing at Angela's inert body. Small toys formed a halo around her head. He rubbed his back, sat down, and dialed 911.

"You mean I have to pay this claim?" Clay asked.

"Yep," Damian answered. "I solved a murder and an embezzlement case."

"I don't give a damn about that."

"Sorry, boss."

Clay let out a long sigh and leaned far back in his chair. "Well, shoot. But a claim is a claim, and that's what we do in this business. I'll write a check today."

ONE WISH

Timothy awakened with a jolt, the pain washing from his front into his spine and creeping up to his neck. He took his medication and gazed out the one window of the hospice room that he shared with his Uncle Martin. *Life isn't fair. I shouldn't be passing away. I'm just a kid! And I lost my mom—I don't even have a memory of her. And even my uncle is dying, too many deaths in such a short life!*

"What are we going to do today, Uncle Martin?" Timothy asked when he saw Martin awakening. With some effort, he lifted himself up and touched his poster of the Phillies team for good luck.

"Well, first we're going to get breakfast, and I'm going to get coffee," Martin replied. "Then, we'll go for a walk in the park. It's supposed to be a nice day." *This dying thing sucks,* he thought. *Stage four pancreatic cancer—a death sentence. What'd I do to deserve that? I'm glad Timothy is here with me; it gives me a purpose in these last few months of life—try to keep life as normal as possible. A losing proposition, to be sure, but a focus.*

The hospice let them share a room since they were related. Timothy was dying of bone cancer. The tragic coincidence of their simultaneous illnesses meant they would spend their last days together, a small consolation; they both had about three months to live.

"Let me help you into your wheelchair," Martin said. "We'll go down to the Schuylkill River Park. Would you like that?"

"Yes!" exclaimed Timothy, pumping his fist. But the gesture tired him, and he lay back in bed to catch his breath.

Timothy was eleven and "nearly five feet tall," as he liked to say, stretching it by a few inches. After the chemotherapy, Timothy had been bald, but he now had a short stubble of tawny hair, which bristled when rubbed. He loved it when his uncle stroked his hair; he could feel Martin's affection. They'd always gotten along well.

The chemo had failed to contain Timothy's cancer because it was too advanced when they discovered it. In addition, the therapy and the illness had left Timothy tired and fragile. Now, he couldn't even walk unassisted.

Timothy's dad, Martin's younger brother, and his stepmom visited each weekend from the suburbs. His mother had died when he was two. Timothy couldn't help feeling cheated—two huge misfortunes in his brief life. But today was Wednesday, and he and Martin would have the day to themselves. His uncle was such a consolation to him.

Martin's fatigue came and went, but today he felt better, bolstered by the drugs. Tall, clear blue eyes, strong limbs, sturdy build, with short-cropped light brown hair, Martin had always been fit, never smoked, and eaten healthy foods, so it shocked him when the doctors told him he had cancer.

As Martin lifted Timothy into his wheelchair, he smelled smoke through the wall.

"I wish Mr. Tanner would stop smoking," Martin said. "He's dying of lung cancer. You'd think the last thing he'd want is another cancer stick." When Martin first caught Tanner smoking in his room, he had complained to the management, who had spoken forcefully to Tanner. They threatened to evict him if he did it again, even though this meant he would die on the streets since he was homeless. This was the first time Mr. Tanner had smoked in his room since that initial incident. Martin pondered the situation but decided to delay reporting Tanner; maybe it was a one-off thing.

Martin and Timothy met him in the hallway on their way to the dining room.

"Don't even start in on me!" Tanner said to Martin. "I have the right to die in my own way."

"Well, just don't take all the rest of us with you by starting a fire," Martin replied.

"We're here to die," Tanner said. "Don't matter how or when." He looked at Timothy and then up at Martin. "That nephew of yours is one ugly son-of-a-bitch."

Timothy's head snapped back, and his eyes widened, but he was too drained to react.

"Don't pay any attention to him, Timothy," Martin said. "He's just scared of dying and he's all alone, without a family."

After breakfast, Martin wheeled Timothy out of the hospice. They spotted Jermaine Telfort, the hardware store owner, across the street, watering his plants. He had worked up a sweat, and his dark skin glistened in the sunlight.

"Good morning!" Jermaine shouted. "Lovely day today!"

They crossed over to chat with him.

"Your flowering plants are beautiful," Martin said.

"Aren't they sweet?" Jermaine said. "They're selling like hotcakes."

"That's good to hear," Martin said.

"We're going to the park!" Timothy said.

"Well, don't let me hold you up. I'm sure you'll see flowers on your way there."

"Wait here, Timothy," Martin said. "I'll get irises for Mrs. McCleary. She doesn't get out much, and I'm sure she'll like them."

Martin picked out a small pot of irises, paid Mr. Telfort, and took them a few doors down the block to Mrs. McCleary's house while Timothy and Mr. Telfort chatted.

After climbing the steps to her porch and knocking on the door, Martin listened to Mrs. McCleary slowly shuffling and scraping her way toward him. She had rheumatoid arthritis, which ran in her family, and had needed a walker for several years.

"Martin!" Mrs. McCleary said when she opened the door. "What a pleasant surprise."

"I brought you flowers," Martin said, handing her the potted plant.

"Oh, you shouldn't have," she said. "Always thinking of others and you with your..." she stopped to wipe a drop from her eye. "I'm so sorry you're ill."

"Oh, don't worry about me, Mrs. McCleary. Timothy and I have each other in the hospice. We're going to the park now."

"You have a good day," Mrs. McCleary said as she patted Martin on the chest while still fighting back the tears.

Mr. Telfort was right; the cherry trees and flowering pear trees were in full blossom. The sun was shining on them, making them luminescent. The warmth of the rays made the flowers give off a sweet scent, almost like there was a trace of powdered sugar in the air. The birds in the trees were chirping happily, flitting from branch to branch. A petal dropped on Timothy's lap, so he tasted it. It had a sour grassy taste with a hint of almond; he spit it out. As they passed a low branch, Martin paused and shook it, sprinkling pink petals down on Timothy, who laughed in delight. Martin grinned as he watched Timothy enjoying the shower.

When they arrived at the park, Martin was tired, so he rolled Timothy onto the grass near the skateboarding playground and sat down beside the chair.

"I wish I could've learned to skateboard," Timothy said. "I'm sorry I never tried it. Now, I'll never get a chance to practice." Tears formed in his eyes.

Martin's throat tightened and his eyes welled up, yet he spoke clearly, "Let's sit here by the river and appreciate the view, the scent of the trees and grass, and the sound of skateboards clacking on the concrete. That's something." And he brushed off a couple more cherry blossoms from Timothy's lap and hugged him.

"Yeah. That is something," Timothy said, looking at the river through the trees and wiping his eyes.

Just then, Martin spotted something shiny in the bushes near where they sat. He rose and picked it out of the dirt. It was a large medallion caked in mud except for one sparkling corner.

"It's a coin," Martin said, showing it to Timothy. "I'll clean it off when we get back to the hospice."

"It's heavy," Timothy said, hefting it.

"Yes, but it's probably not worth anything. No one could lose such a large medal." Martin felt a tingle in his fingers as he put the coin away. *What if it's something special? But I don't want to give Timothy any false hopes.*

When they returned to their room, a lovely flowering plant was on Timothy's nightstand. They both agreed to thank Mr. Telfort the following day.

With Timothy safely tucked into bed that evening, Martin washed the coin in their sink. The dirt came off quickly, revealing a plain-looking metal disk with two words written on both sides: "Rub me."

"Humph. Isn't that the darndest thing?" Martin said to himself, his stomach tightening.

"What?" Timothy asked.

"Oh, nothing. It's just a boring old coin." Martin locked it in the night table next to his bed, where he kept his diary, his hands shaking. Then he settled himself under his covers, his palms sweating, his brow deeply furrowed. *Could the coin be magic?*

"Hey, Timothy? What would you have wanted to do with your life aside from skateboarding?"

"Uh, I dunno," Timothy said, but then he spotted his poster of the Phillies. "I guess I always wanted to be great at baseball. I dreamed of being in the major leagues when I played in the Little League."

"That would've been nice. I would have wished that also. I could go to the stadium and tell the other fans, 'That's my nephew.'" Martin leaned over and ruffled the hair at the back of Timothy's head, causing the boy to giggle gleefully.

With those thoughts, they fell into a deep sleep.

In the middle of the night, the fire alarms went off. Smoke was everywhere. Martin leaped out of bed and went to the door, but the handle was too hot to open. He rushed to the window, threw it open, picked up Timothy, and helped him outside, lowering him carefully so he could hold on to the window ledge before falling back onto the grass. Then, he jumped out after him and carried him across the street to where Jermaine was standing, setting him on the chair near the shop's door.

"Are you two alright?" Jermaine asked, his voice cracking.

"We're fine, now that we're with you," Martin said. Then he looked back at their window and remembered the coin.

"I've got to save my diary!" he yelled, not wanting to mention the medallion. "It's about all I have."

"The fire department will be here soon," Jermaine said.

"No! I'm going back in!"

Jermaine tried to grab Martin, but it was too late; Martin was already running back to the window he had exited with Timothy. Martin jumped through the opening, landing in a heap on the floor. He coughed and couldn't open his eyes because the smoke was so thick. How was he going to find his nightstand?

With his eyes shut, his throat burning, and his whole body dripping with sweat from the heat, Martin crawled to where he thought he would find his bed. He reached out his hand to touch his bedside table, but all he felt was a burning-hot wall. Martin jerked back his arm so forcefully that he fell backward, bumping his head on a bed. He realized it must be Timothy's, so he scuttled backward until he found his bed and sidled around it to where the table had to be. He grabbed his diary and stuffed the coin in his pocket.

And then he fainted.

When he gained consciousness moments later, his nose was pressed to the floor, and he was breathing fresh air from the window. He took a deep breath and launched himself toward the breeze, leaping at the last second to pitch his body through the opening; he hit the wall instead, crumpling to the floor.

Jermaine thought he saw Martin trying to get out, so he ran to the window, reached in, and grabbed Martin by his collar. Martin pushed, Jermaine pulled and together they got Martin out of the building. They staggered to safety across the road.

Soon, the fire department arrived and quickly extinguished the fire. The fire chief reprimanded Martin for going back into the burning building. Martin apologized; Jermaine consoled him.

Mr. Tanner, who must've fallen asleep smoking, had started the fire. The blaze reached the hallway but was mostly confined to his and Timothy and Martin's room. He died of smoke inhalation, the only casualty at the hospice.

The next day, Timothy and Martin were assigned another room. The fire had destroyed all their belongings, but Timothy's parents brought them fresh attire.

That evening, they settled into their new accommodation, which looked exactly like the old one. They were exhausted from missing sleep the night before. Timothy fell fast asleep, but Martin was restless. He kept thinking about the coin. Could it be like Aladdin's lamp? He took it out of his drawer.

He reread the inscription and thought about it for a long time, growing drowsy. Then, having finally decided, he rubbed the disk between both hands. There was a flash of light, and Martin looked up to see a woman clothed all in white. Her light brown skin and dress glowed, illuminating the entire room. Martin looked over at Timothy, but he was still sleeping soundly.

"I am the Fairy of the Coin," the apparition said. "The Coin seeks individuals pure of heart. It grants them one wish when it finds them and then disappears to seek another worthy soul. The Coin has found you; you have one wish."

Martin couldn't believe his eyes or ears. He was dumbstruck and didn't know what to do. The fairy continued to shimmer in the dim room. Its iridescent light made his eyelids grow heavier and heavier, but he had one fleeting thought before he slipped into a profound slumber.

The following day, Martin leapt out of bed. He hadn't felt this good in months. He and Timothy went to breakfast, and he was happy to see Timothy's appetite was robust; the boy ate everything on his plate and asked for an extra egg.

A few weeks passed, and Martin's strength surprised him; he felt rejuvenated. Timothy was also getting stronger.

One day, Timothy got out of his wheelchair and walked across the room. He hadn't been able to do that for months. Within another week, Timothy could walk to the food hall unassisted. The hospice staff took him to the hospital for tests. His blood count was improving. Could the cancer be in remission? Timothy wished that with all his might.

Sure enough, within two months of Martin's late-night visit from the fairy, Timothy was sufficiently healthy to return home. His parents came to pick him up, and Martin gave him a long goodbye hug.

A week later, Martin's health turned suddenly for the worse. Timothy and his parents visited him in a special section of the hospice, but it was clear he was dying.

"Here, Timothy," Martin said, "take this key to my drawer. I'd like you to have my diary and that old coin. Both are in my nightstand."

Timothy and his parents went to Martin's room to retrieve the items on their way out. But when Timothy opened the drawer, he found only the journal. The medallion was nowhere to be seen.

The next day, they learned Martin had died quietly in the night. Timothy and his parents gathered Martin's personal effects, and as they were leaving the hospice, Timothy saw Mr. Telfort tending to his trees and bushes. Timothy went over to say goodbye.

"Hey, Mr. Telfort," Timothy said. "Uncle Martin..." Timothy faltered, tears flooding his eyes.

"Yes, I know, I heard already," Jermaine said, and he bent over and embraced Timothy, who sobbed on his shoulder.

"Your uncle was a kind, generous man. The best of the best. You should always remember him and honor him by being like him. He always lent a helping hand to those who needed it; he would've given anything to have you get well. And, now, here you are, walking home a young, healthy man."

"I will. I'll honor him." Then Timothy noticed all the plants.

"After the fire, I forgot to thank you for the flowers you gave me," Timothy said. "I didn't get to enjoy them long."

"Think nothing of it. I'm so happy you are better now."

A year passed, and one day after Timothy's baseball practice, he came home to grab his skateboard to go to the park.

"Timothy," his stepmom said, "you be careful. I don't want you to get hurt."

"I know, Mom. I'm always careful," he said as he dashed out the door.

One of the kid's boards was broken at the park, so Timothy shared his board with him until it was close to dark. Before leaving, Timothy walked over to the grassy knoll where he and his uncle had sat down to rest. It seemed so long ago. He resolved to read his uncle's diary again. His uncle had seemed so concerned about it the night of the fire, but when Timothy read it, he thought it was dull; it was all about the weather, their health, what they did that day. It was OK to recall some of their outings, but it wasn't that interesting, so he had set it aside and forgotten about it.

Just before going to bed, Timothy got out the journal. As he opened it, a bright glow outside his window startled him, causing him to drop the book. He ran to the window, opened it, and looked out. Was that a shiny edge of a dress disappearing around the corner of the house? He wasn't sure.

Timothy turned back into his room and picked up the diary, shaking his head in bewilderment. A folded slip of paper dropped out of a compartment at the back that he hadn't noticed before. He opened it and read:

Dear Timothy,
If you're reading this, you're safe at home and healthy. I am so happy for you. I hope you know that I always wished you'd have a long, healthy future. I would have traded my life for that.
Your loving uncle,
Martin

Timothy knelt in front of the window and looked out into the night; he wanted to thank his uncle.

"Dear Uncle Martin. I don't know what happened at the hospice, but I know I'm alive today because of you. Thank you."

He sent his gratitude into the vastness of the sky. He felt a warm pulse in his chest and knew that his uncle was in a good place and was happy. A flash in the heavens caught his eye; he saw a vision of a woman dressed in shimmering white floating amongst the stars. She was smiling, nodding, and holding a glowing coin in her outstretched hand.

THE TRANSYLVANIAN CABINET

C hadwell Poole lifted the box of wood from near the door and strode out into the cool, gray late-winter afternoon. At least it wasn't raining. He was renting a room in a row house in the Logan Square area of Philadelphia specifically because it was near an excellent cabinetmaker. The box had arrived the day before, and it had all the pieces he needed for his cabinet. The wood was a rare species from the Hoia Baciu Forest in Transylvania.

Chadwell stepped into the store.

"Hello. How can I help you?" the proprietor asked.

"I would like you to build me a cabinet with the wood I provide you. I've double-checked, and all the pieces you need are here in this box."

"Great! Thanks for dropping by. I'm Chip Dawson, by the way."

"Chadwell Poole, at your service," he said while thinking what a delightfully absurd name Chip was for a cabinetmaker. They shook hands.

Chadwell looked around the room. Wood was everywhere: on the floor, stacked on shelves, and on benches. The large window at the front displayed finished products, including small vases, a chessboard, animal figures, and various wooden knickknacks. A large worktable, covered with assorted tools, filled the middle of the floor. The chaos of the shop unsettled Chadwell, but he steeled himself and looked at Chip, who was medium height with broad shoulders, fair complexion, sandy hair, and blue eyes. He was wearing a pair of jeans with a few holes in them and a long-sleeved black T-shirt with a crew collar.

"Here are the specifications," Chadwell said. Chadwell had measured everything three times and, though he was not a carpenter, he knew the pieces could make the cabinet he desired.

"It looks like you have wood joints throughout. I could make it with screws and it would be a lot cheaper and quicker to build."

"No. It absolutely must have wooden joints as specified: a dovetail here, a miter there, and bridle joints on the door frame."

"It says you want colorless glass for the door. You mean clear?" Chip asked.

"The glass should be of the highest quality and as colorless as possible."

"We could get museum glass. It's unmatched for clarity, blocks out ultraviolet light, and has little or no reflection, so it looks invisible."

"That would be perfect!" Chadwell said, clapping his small hands in front of him.

Chip regarded his customer. Chadwell was short, with a slight build, his graying hair mostly hidden by a fedora, set at a rakish angle on his small head. The man was brown in every way: eyes, face, aging spots on his hands, and a brown herringbone suit with a waistcoat. His shoes were highly polished, and he had a gold chain for his pocket watch stretching from the buttonhole of his waistcoat to its right pocket. In short, he was dressed impeccably. His accent was English.

"An odd duck," thought Chip, but he liked the man instantly.

"How long will it take?" asked Chadwell, his voice almost squeaking.

"Well, a couple of months at least. I must make sure the wood is properly cured, then I need to plan out the entire project, deciding which joints to glue first..."

"No glue! There should be absolutely no glue used on the joints and the finish should be natural coconut oil. And I'll supply the hinges and knob to complete the project."

"Ok. That will take longer and cost more, but I can do that." Chip liked the idea of making a cabinet without screws and glue; it required skills he rarely used.

"That's why I came to you, Mr. Dawson, because you are one of the best, if not *the* best, cabinetmaker in Philadelphia," Chadwell said, clasping his hands in front of him and beaming like a five-year-old. "And money is no object."

"Please. Call me Chip," Chip said with a shy grin, his chest warming as it puffed out. "Why don't you come back tomorrow, and I'll give you a detailed quote and timeline?"

"That would be most satisfactory," said Chadwell and he strode out into the now sunny day, his chin held high.

After dinner with his landlords, Mr. and Mrs. Halliwell, Chadwell took the stairs to his room on the third floor. The home-cooked meal, "comfort food" it was called, of beef stew was enhanced by a bottle of Sangiovese that he had bought to celebrate the beginning of his project. The food was perfectly adequate, but nothing compared to his Beef Wellington. He missed having a place—and a kitchen—of his own, but the rebuilt cabinet would solve that problem. Too bad he couldn't rush the project, but Chip had assured him he would finish it as soon as possible and exactly as specified.

His room was furnished with an easy chair, a desk, a bed, and a closet; the wallpaper pattern featured faded red roses. Chadwell rummaged in the crate containing the remains of the former cabinet. He had already removed all the glass and disposed of it, but he was reluctant to discard the valuable wood; perhaps Mr. Dawson could make some use of it. He pulled out what was left of the door and removed the hinges, knob, and screws.

They were all made of sterling silver. He sat down at his desk and began polishing them.

After about two months, Chip contacted Chadwell and told him everything was ready; he just needed the hinges to complete the job. Chadwell gathered them up and headed over to Chip's shop. Chip was waiting for him when Chadwell entered and handed him the hardware.

"They're silver?" Chip asked.

"Yes!" Chadwell said with a broad grin on his face.

"OK. It may take a couple of hours to attach them. The fitting must be exact, so the door opens horizontally."

"I understand," said Chadwell. "I'll take a walk and be back in two hours. After you have finished the door, don't open it! I must absolutely be the first person to open the cabinet."

"OK." Chip said slowly, his brow wrinkling.

Precisely two hours later, Chadwell returned. The cabinet was still on its back on the worktable, but the door was attached.

"Do you want to test the door?" Chip asked.

"No, I'll do that at home," Chadwell said, his eyes wide as he gazed at the cabinet. "I'll call a cab; I don't want to break it again."

"Oh, don't do that. It's only three blocks away; I'll drive you over. Just wait here while I fetch my truck."

"Thank you. That is so awfully kind of you."

"It's nothing."

When Chip returned with his pickup, they gently wrapped the cabinet in a blanket, loaded it into the back, and secured it. Soon, they were in front of the Halliwell's row house and carefully took the cabinet up to Chadwell's room.

"Thank you, sir, for your most excellent service! I'm indebted to you."

"No," Chip said. "You paid me in full." They shook hands and Chip departed.

Chadwell listened as the cabinetmaker closed the door behind him, and he heard the vehicle depart. Even though the Halliwells were out shopping for dinner, he locked his door.

He turned and looked at the tabletop cabinet built with a wood so dark it looked black in the dim lighting. It was about three feet high and a foot-and-a-half wide, with the beveled top hanging over the front and sides by about a half-inch. It stood on four-inch legs and had a single glass door with silver fittings.

He opened the door slowly. "Sapphire! How lovely to see you!" For there, standing a full eight-inches tall, was a fairy, with her arms folded over her tiny chest and her wings flapping vigorously.

"Where have you been?" Sapphire said with a slight Slavic accent. "I've been in limbo for months; I don't even know for how long!"

"The shippers dropped the container with our furniture and the only thing damaged was this cabinet," Chadwell said. "I had it repaired as fast as possible, but you can't rush quality."

"Humph," Sapphire said, tossing her golden hair back to get it out of her emerald-green eyes. "It is a nice cabinet; it even smells pleasant. Coconut? Everything is the same as before except the wood is new," Sapphire said, as she flew out of the cabinet to inspect the exterior.

"Yes, it is as good as new and no glue or artificial anything. A beautiful home for you."

"Yes, it's most agreeable," Sapphire said, as she settled into a sitting position on the single shelf in the middle of the cupboard.

"I was wondering if we could talk about my annual wish?" Chadwell asked.

"Oh, yes, it's always about you and your wish. Never about me and my needs!"

"But I had this lovely cabinet built for you, my dear."

"Yes. I suppose. And it is quite satisfying. OK. It can't be too excessive; we mustn't draw attention to ourselves. What is it?"

"What I'd like is sufficient money to buy a condo in a high-rise with a southwestern view and a trust fund for my living expenses; nothing extravagant, just to make me comfortable. We're saving lots of money by choosing Philadelphia rather than New York."

"It's always something for you," Sapphire said. "Why don't you do something for the cabinetmaker? He did such an excellent job and I'm back!"

"Perhaps I could take him and his wife out to dinner, but that doesn't preclude my wish."

"True. But what about something more altruistic? There are a lot of refugees in Philadelphia from Afghanistan, Ukraine, everywhere! Some nutjob in Texas is even sending people here from Latin America. You should wish for homes for them, not yourself!"

"How do you know about all that?" Chadwell asked. "I thought you were in limbo."

"I was, but even in that godforsaken nothingness space, I tapped into all the air transmissions, and I sensed we were in the Philadelphia area. You know I always keep abreast of global developments."

"Yes, that's why I subscribe to the Financial Times, so I can keep up with you."

"Whatever," Sapphire said. "I really think you should help the immigrants this year. And take the Dawsons to dinner!"

"Yes, my love. Perhaps we can talk about this another time. I hear the Halliwells calling me to dinner."

"That's fine. I'll be attending a party in Fairydustville. Don't wait up for me."

"Of course, my dear."

Chadwell grabbed the bottle of Châteauneuf-du-Pape he had purchased for the evening's meal and descended to greet the Halliwells. With the wine complimenting the pot roast, the dinner was a festive affair.

The next day, Chadwell arranged with Chip to take him and his wife to dinner that evening at a steak house near Rittenhouse Square. Then he took a walk in the sunny, spring day. The cherry and pear trees were blossoming; the Logan Square neighborhood was full of their pink and white splendor.

Oh, but what to do about this year's wish? The immigrants were certainly deserving; and more in need than he was, he had to admit. Sapphire was right; the immigrants should come first. He feared, however, that next year would be the same—like it had been in London. There was always someone or a cause more worthy than him. He didn't want anything extravagant, simply a comfortable life. Was that too much to ask? Owning the cabinet—which he inherited from his aunt in Romania—with its resident fairy, was like being in charge of a foundation with a modest endowment; each year, in consultation with Sapphire, he would wish for a donation of about three million dollars for a laudable charity. Sapphire always "lifted" the funds from Caribbean accounts of nefarious oligarchs. Surely, the manager of such a foundation warranted remuneration? Anyway, it was dreary living at the Halliwells. Yes, they were nice; the food was good, and the room cozy, but Chadwell longed for a place of his own and to cook for himself again! He hadn't realized how much he missed his time in the kitchen until it was gone.

Chadwell and the Dawsons arrived at a pleasant restaurant near Rittenhouse Square at the same time, meeting outside the front door of the posh eatery.

After introducing his wife, Alice, Chip said, "You really needn't take us to dinner, Mr. Poole. I was delighted to make the cabinet for you."

"Nonsense. You did a fabulous job and restored it to its former glory. I'm exceedingly pleased with it. And call me Chadwell."

"OK. If you insist."

At the dinner table, the conversation turned to—of all things—the immigrants arriving in Philadelphia from around the world.

"Yes, when we heard of all these unfortunate people from Afghanistan who had helped our armed forces in their country, we couldn't say 'no' to taking in a mother and her daughter," Alice said.

"You have two refugees living with you?" Chadwell asked, his mouth dropping open.

"Yes," said Chip. "We're learning a lot from them about their culture and helping Zahra look for a job. She was a translator and speaks English fluently but has few other skills."

"It's a tough city, Philadelphia," Alice said. "There is a lot of poverty and too many homeless people."

"Yes, we also help at Philabundance once a week, helping cook or serve food to those less well-off than ourselves," Chip said.

"My, you are such fine people," Chadwell said. "I'm very impressed with your sense of social responsibility." Chadwell's thoughts turned toward his dilemma over his next wish.

Perhaps he really should follow Sapphire's advice? His stomach turned, his head bent, and his shoulders slumped.

"Are you alright, Chadwell?" Chip asked.

"Yes, I'm fine," Chadwell said, straightening. "I was just thinking about all these people in need. Perhaps I could do something as well..."

"Sadly, there is plenty to do," Alice said. "But it can be very rewarding. Chip and I can't have children, so we are delighted to have Samira and her mother Zahra in our home."

"Yes, I'm sure," Chadwell said, but his voice was faint.

The next morning, Chadwell opened the cabinet to speak to Sapphire, but she was still fast asleep after partying at another Fairyland event. But, by evening he could hear her wings fluttering in her home, which by now Sapphire had furnished with a formal sitting room below and a kitchen, dining area and playroom on the shelf above. Chip had cut a hole for passage between the two. Curtains on the glass door provided privacy.

Chadwell poured himself a glass of Burgundy, got out his eyedropper, and opened the cabinet.

"Good evening, Sapphire? Care for a glass of wine?"

"Oh, surely. Thank you, Chadwell."

Chadwell dipped his dropper into his glass and sucked out a bit of wine. Sapphire retrieved a glass and Chadwell filled it with several drops.

"Thank you," Sapphire said. "Delightful!"

"My dinner with the Dawsons went very well; they thoroughly enjoyed their meal and the evening with me."

"Excellent."

"I was wondering if we could discuss this year's wish tonight?"

"Absolutely. I'm sure you've come to your senses and decided to help those less fortunate than yourself."

"Yes, I have. You are absolutely right to put the immigrants first."

"I am?"

"The Dawsons and I discussed the situation in Philadelphia last night, and I believe that is the right thing to do."

"You do? What about your condo and trust fund?"

"That will just have to wait."

"My, my, my, this is an unexpected development," Sapphire said. "But perhaps we could still do something for you..."

"That really isn't necessary. I'll be perfectly fine here with the Halliwells."

"I know," Sapphire said. "But what if we had two wishes in one year and skipped next year?"

"You'd do that for me? But what would the Grand Fairy say?"

"I'll go to her shortly. But first, another glass of that excellent wine."

"Of course, my dear," said Chadwell and refilled her empty goblet.

"I'm off!"

"Safe flight!" Chadwell said as he watched Sapphire vanish in a swirl of flapping wings.

Chadwell poured himself another glass of wine and settled into the comfy armchair. It's not *sooo* bad here, he said to himself before nodding off.

Some while later, a commotion awakened him. Sapphire was shouting in his ear in her tiny voice, her wings beating furiously behind her.

"We can do it! We can do it!" she said, her voice singing the phrase.

"That's fabulous. Thank you!" Chadwell said as he repositioned himself in his chair, a rosy glow on his cheeks. He blew a kiss at Sapphire and she returned it with both hands, then disappeared into her cabinet, closing the door behind her.

"Well, that's that!" thought Chadwell, emitting a long, contented sigh. "Support for the immigrants, and a home for me."

Up in Fairydustville, the Grand Fairy smiled. She knew all along that when she broke the cabinet, Chadwell would meet Chip and Alice.

MODERN ROMANCE: NYC

"I'll be wearing black, so it'll be easy to spot me," Sue said toward the end of their first call.

"OK, I'll be in black and white, so I should also be easy to find," Hank said.

"Maybe you don't know New York very well. Everyone wears black. Especially women wear black, so that was a small joke. No one in New York wears any white in autumn."

"Yes, I knew it was a joke, so it was black-and-white back at you, as in old movies. You said you had a background in films."

"Clever, but sly. At least you're a cute sneak, judging from your photo on Match. Thank you for introducing me to Jim Hall. 'Deep in a Dream' was a delightful selection. I love delicate and evocative guitar playing. I'll send your first song via email: Sara Bareilles's 'Gravity.'"

"Thanks. I'm looking forward to that and to meeting you on Saturday," Hank said.

Hank arrived early at the French restaurant he'd chosen on the West Side of Midtown Manhattan, checked in with the hostess, took a seat at the bar, and ordered a Sancerre. He spotted Sue in the bar mirror as soon as she entered. She was tall, maybe six feet, slim, and with wavy dark brown hair. After speaking to the maître d', she turned toward the bar and cast a radiant smile in Hank's direction.

"You really are in black and white!" she exclaimed as she reached the bar and took a seat next to him.

"As I said I would be," he said. "Can I order you a glass of Sancerre? Our table's not ready for another half hour."

"Sure, that'd be great."

He gazed at her in the mirror as he ordered the wine. She was younger-looking than he expected and stunning, but in a shy, nervous way. She was wearing a simple black dress with a white scarf, complementing his black cashmere sport coat, white shirt, and dark gray slacks. He hoped his nervous anticipation wasn't too evident.

"True confession: I googled you. Thanks for giving me your last name on the phone the other day, Sue."

"Again, you prove yourself to be a cunning guy. I'm going to have to be careful around you. And, you never told me *your* last name."

"You seem to be very accomplished at film editing. You've tons of work out there, though most are indie films."

"Hmmm. Pumping me for information, but I still don't know your last name."

"Sorry, I tend not to say it too early when I meet people because then they think that it's my first name. My name's Hank Terry, and if you want to google me, *'Hank Terry, economist'* works."

"Interesting. You'd think that with a name like Susan Robin, I'd have thought to hold back my last name too. But, hey, we both have two first names. That's karma, no?"

"Yes, of a sort," he said, laughing. "I sometimes even have people I've known for a long time call me 'Terry.'"

"I know! I hate it when that happens. Last week, I was called 'Robin' by my hairdresser. I should book my appointments as 'Susan R.' Also, someone in my Ph.D. program did the same thing recently."

"Sorry. But how is your Ph.D. in Education coming along? That's a major shift in careers."

"What I like most is working with children. I'm enjoying my part-time job teaching first graders. I just love seeing life through their eyes. They're so fresh, so innocent. The Ph.D. itself is going fine, but lots of work."

"Cool. Maybe you can become a principal at a lower school and do substitute teaching from time to time? Or, stay in academia and still have a teaching gig."

"I've not sorted that out yet, I admit."

"Though you've a lot of credits for film editing, you seem to have only one screenplay, so I put *Ledge of Fear* at the top of my Netflix list."

"Let me make this very clear and simple. If you watch *Ledge of Fear*, I'll never speak to you again."

"Gee, Sue, I'm getting the vague impression you don't want me to watch your film."

"It's totally humiliating to be associated with something so appallingly bad. There's a long, interesting story behind it, but I'll only relay it if you don't watch it!"

"OK. That's straightforward. I'll delete it from my list."

"And what about you, Dr. Economist? Tell me about your work."

"Why don't I pay up here, and we can go to our table?"

As they got seated, he replied, "Well, you know, I'm an economist working at an insurance company...so, before your eyes roll too far back in your head, all I can say is, I find it very interesting."

"Yes, but what do you do?"

"We do PR, strategic, and marketing support. So, for me, a lot of writing, editing, forecasting, managing staff, learning about insurance markets, and speaking at conferences and with clients. I sometimes deal with the press as part of the PR work. So, I'm often a talking head with my name and my company's name underneath."

Sue googled him. "OK. Yes. There you are on Bloomberg. I'll watch it later. You're overly modest. And your personal life—have you ever been married?"

"Married twice, divorced twice, one daughter each marriage. No regrets. You?"

"You've said that line before."

"I have."

"As for me, I was married, but it wasn't working. However, we remain friends."

Hank found Sue to be intelligent, interesting, engaging, and very pretty. She liked to tease but only in a fun way. He couldn't believe his luck when she said that she was also eager to meet again.

"That was a delightful dinner. I'm so glad we met," Hank said. "I'd like to meet again, and I don't know about you, but I'm looking for a long-term relationship with full commitment. But, first, it'd be smart, of course, to get to know each other better."

"That's so funny—and charming—that you mention that. I wanted to bring up the same topic. Yes. I also am looking for something long-term. So, we've that in common as well."

"Great! Unfortunately, I've a lot of work-related travel coming up. I'm in Beijing and Australia over the Thanksgiving holidays. Then off to London and Zurich the following weekend," he said.

"I'm also traveling. I fly out Friday, return on Tuesday the 30th. I'll miss my kids, but I need to see my father. He's having an operation," she said.

"Well, that's certainly important. I hope all goes well. Unfortunately, it looks like the earliest we can reconnect is Saturday, the eleventh of December. Does that work for you?" Hank said, gazing at the calendar on his phone.

"Yes, I have it on my calendar already, and I'm looking forward to it."

They gathered their things and headed out onto the street. Hank hailed a cab for her. After it arrived, as he held the door open, she threw her arms around his neck and kissed him sweetly on the lips, startling him.

"Ooh. I see you're not used to PDA," she smiled, got in the cab, and waved as it pulled away.

He had to admit he was blushing a bit; he wasn't used to public displays of affection. But the evening had gone exceedingly well. He'd stay in touch via email and phone calls while they both traveled.

The trip to Sydney and Beijing went well for Hank. He had a little extra time in Sydney, so he went to his favorite museums, The Art Gallery of New South Wales and the Museum of Contemporary Art. As always, he walked everywhere. It's a healthy way to get around and very doable in downtown Sydney.

He spent almost his entire time in Beijing working, but he squeezed in enough time to go to the Pearl Market to buy jewelry for his daughters. The Pearl Market is a big, sprawling indoor market housed in one building in the Chongwen District of Beijing. Electronics, T-shirts, handicrafts, shoes, clothes, food, toys, and lots of jewelry, especially pearls, are sold by hundreds of different merchants. The pearls are mostly freshwater cultured pearls, but they still look pretty and come in various colors—pink, white, black. On a previous trip, he bought his daughters white and black pearl necklaces, but for Zora, he chose coral, which she loves, and for Jenna, a necklace with mixed stones. When he got back to the US, he'd look for an additional gift for them. He thought about getting something for Sue, but decided the inexpensive pearl strands wouldn't do.

While Hank traveled, he stayed in touch with Sue through amusing, bantering emails. Also, they traded songs: he sent Chet Baker and Keely Smith. She sent Fiona Apple's "Criminal," Norah Jones singing "A Foggy Day in London Town," and Amy Winehouse's "Rehab." Amy and Fiona were a challenge for him, but Norah's tune was familiar.

One of Hank's emails caused upset. Hank had forgotten that after he'd scheduled the first date with Sue, but before they met, he'd accepted a third date with someone who had bought tickets for them at a Carnegie Hall concert. When his email revealed this, Sue wasn't impressed and let him know in her responding email. So, Hank phoned her from his hotel in Zurich.

"Sue, it's Hank. Do you have time to talk?"

"Oh, yes. It's nice that you're honest and open, and, of course, there's no obligation, but I thought we had an understanding, and that was reinforced—for me—by the emails and phone calls. Now, I hear you have a Match date on the day before we meet at the Algonquin. Why don't you just take Emily there also? I'm not sure I'd feel comfortable on Saturday thinking that you were comparing me to her."

"I'm sorry I wasn't clear. I'm only interested in you. The person I'll see on Friday is someone I've been out with twice. I met her before I met you. We went on two dates, and she then bought concert tickets for us at Carnegie Hall on the tenth."

"Hmmm. She must really like you."

"Perhaps, but when I met you, I was smitten. I still am, but I figured the odds of you being interested in me were ten percent—despite positive signals from you. I'm flabbergasted and flattered you're attracted to me."

"You've no clue how attractive you are. I find you irresistible."

"Thank you. You're very kind, but you're younger, beautiful, you've done some exciting things in your life, and you continue to do valuable and fascinating work. After my second date with Emily, she bought the tickets. Now that I know you're interested in me, I'll phone Emily and clarify that I've met someone, but I'd like to be friends if she's agreeable. She may choose not to see me. That's fair also. But, to reiterate, it's you, only you, I'm interested in."

"From my viewpoint," Sue said, "I'm just not willing to return to duplicitous relationships filled with the accompanying anger and upset."

"Agreed. I've been there too. All I can say is that I'll always be honest and faithful as long as we're together."

"OK. Thank you for that. I'm sorry for jumping to conclusions."

"No. Perfectly understandable. It was a poorly written email. Look, we clearly could benefit from more time together. If you're available, we could also meet on the ninth if you like."

"I thought that was the day you were returning from London?"

"It is, but I arrive back early and can recover in the afternoon. How about a light dinner and an early evening? It'd be super to catch up and see each other, rather than phone calls and emails. How about Mexican food and we can meet at seven p.m.?"

"Great. I love Mexican food. Until then."

After hanging up, Hank breathed a sigh of relief. To celebrate, he drank a whiskey from the minibar before going to bed.

The work and travel made the days pass quickly. The emails involved a lot of teasing and chatting and usually included the exchange of songs. He sent more Chet and Les Paul with Mary Ford singing "Prisoner of Love." She responded with more of Sara B. and Amy W.

The ninth came and, predictably, the Mexican place was packed, but they had a reservation, and the hostess found a reasonably quiet table on the upper floor.

"How'd your talk go in London?"

"It went well. Only one person fell asleep out of twenty. I've found that five percent of the audience will invariably be asleep soon after I start talking."

"That's impressive! I'm so happy for you that it was only five percent. The real statistic is that twenty percent of the population are sleep-deprived, so you kept seventy-five percent of those souls awake. You should bask in the glory of your almost-snooze-free event."

"I like your way of looking at it. Hey, I've been trying to find *Ledge of Fear*—the book, not the movie—to read, but failing miserably."

"Ack! If you're sure you want to read it, maybe I'll lend you a copy. *Ledge of Fear* began as a tender story about an obscure folk singer, Amelia Desert. It should never have been a film, but the shame is that the film didn't reflect Amelia's life the way she saw it. Sad. She was more invested in the project than I was, and it came out badly. She liked my script because it was her story, but the director made the film he wanted, focusing more on her life's negative parts. The book, as well as the movie, has some ugly scenes."

"For us," she continued, "I'd hope we can stay in a more peaceful place. I've had enough anger and upset in my life and don't care to go down that path again."

"Yes. I'm the same way."

"Which reminds me, I hope you found time to have fun in London?"

"Yes, I saw friends on Friday night and went to the Tate Britain on Saturday but flew back to Zurich and worked on Sunday. You?"

"Well, mostly work, work, work, but the students in my program had a party last night. They make any excuse to have a party, and it was Megan's birthday. The other students are so accepting of me, even though I'm much older. It's so sweet."

"Maybe that's because you look so young and are young at heart."

"Thank you. You *are* adorable. Anyway, it was amusing and a pleasant break from all the coursework."

"I almost hate to bring it up, but I talked to Emily, and she still wants to meet tomorrow and seems amenable to being friends."

"OK. Don't have too much fun tomorrow."

"Absolutely. No fun whatsoever. Zero. Zilch. Nada. Guaranteed."

"That's good to hear."

This time, the PDA came before Hank could call a cab. Sue hugged him and gave him a long, lingering kiss, followed by a tight hug and a sigh.

"It's good to know the physical attraction is there, also," she said.

As they separated, he said, "Yes. I'll see you at the Algonquin on Saturday."

"I'll bring my favorite Dorothy Parker quotes. Until the eleventh, my loveable economist."

As was his custom, Hank reached the Algonquin early. In working for a Swiss insurance company, Hank had learned to be overly punctual, arriving promptly everywhere. To his surprise, Sue showed up only moments after he sat down.

"So, I forgot to ask about your father on Thursday. Jetlag, I guess. How did his operation go?"

"Everything went fine. It was good to be with my dad, helping him to recuperate from the surgery. Also, my sister stopped by for a day with her two sons. So, it was great to catch up with her. We don't see each other often. My nephews are both musical, so they gave us a concert. Alex, the older one, played the piano and Michael the violin. To top it off, my dad's become somewhat more liberal as he ages, so the family get-togethers go a lot more smoothly these days. I'm not sure why he's evolved, but it's so pleasant because we can talk about politics and not just about the weather."

"Yes, several days talking only about the weather, especially in New Mexico, could be a bit dry. Does the weather ever change?"

"That was an awful pun."

"Agreed. Sorry."

"Occasionally, one does see a cloud. Sometimes it rains."

"I know. My mother used to live in Santa Fe, and I went there regularly, sometimes with my two daughters."

"Oh, yes, tell me about your daughters!"

"I always say: 'My two top accomplishments in life are Zora and Jenna,'" he said while holding up his right hand and counting off the achievements with his fingers.

"That's sweet."

"They're doing extremely well. They both did well with their first degrees and seem to have no trouble finding jobs. So, no worries for Dad! We get along well. I took them on some holidays after my divorce so they could get to know each other better since they're six years apart. The younger one hates it when I tease her, so I'm trying to cut back on that. In any case, she's learned to push back, while Zora ignores me when I tease. I mean it to be humorous, but sometimes it may have some bite. That reminds me. Zora will visit me this coming week for two whole days, which is quite a treat for me. I got a couple of tickets to *Fela!* so we'll be able to see that together."

"I enjoyed that musical. It's so vibrant! I hope Zora enjoys it also."

"How about you? Did you ever want to have kids?"

"No, I never had that as a goal, and my former husband and I were very consumed with work."

"Shame. I'm sure you'd have been an amazing mother."

"Thank you. That's very generous of you to say that."

Hank and Sue listened to the singer, who was perhaps beyond her prime but singing delightful Christmas tunes.

Afterward, outside, Hank commented, "I'm not sure about the chanteuse, but the food and company were splendid."

"Oh, she was fun. But I must admit I'm tired, so I need to get home and get some sleep. I'm glad we can look forward to seeing each other next Friday. You're coming to my place, and I'll pretend to make dinner for us. Afterward, we'll watch *Wall Street* and you can explain all the financial dealings to me. Bring your pajamas. That's the only way to watch a movie at home."

"Oookaay. I like that. Pajamas. Noted."

"And a final Dorothy P quote for you: 'Brevity is the soul of lingerie.' Think about it."

"I am. Definitely."

And then another endless kiss, and she was gone.

During the week, Zora came to New York from Philadelphia, where she was studying to get her MBA. Hank and she enjoyed *Fela!* and had a second night together at a restaurant. Hank was pleased to learn that everything was going well for her in her studies. He was also delighted to see how happy she was when she talked about her latest boyfriend, and he told Zora he hoped it proved to be everything she wished for.

The weekend finally arrived. Hank had been careful to check in with Sue during the week because she seemed anxious about cooking. Before going to her apartment on the Upper West Side, he was to pick up salmon from his local fish market. It was a cold, clear evening, so he took the subway up to Columbus Circle and walked the rest of the way. New York at night in winter is magical, and that's how Hank felt. The crowd at the Circle was much more friendly and festive than usual. New York at its best. Sue'd even gotten tickets to Dizzy's for next week for them, so there was that to look forward to as well.

After reaching her floor, he saw her door was ajar, so he knocked and entered. She rushed over to him and greeted him with a delightful kiss and hug.

"What a lovely welcome. Thank you! Here's the fish, and I'm happy to help with the cooking. I'm a decent cook, you know."

"I bet you are, among other talents. Thanks for getting the salmon. I'm just going to cook it *en papillote* with fennel, zucchini, and lemon slices and dill on top. We'll have *sautéed* potatoes on the side. Does that sound good?"

"It sounds way better than good. I thought you implied you didn't know how to cook?"

"It's a very simple recipe. You can slice the fennel and the zucchini, and I'll work on the paper casing and potatoes."

They happily prepared the meal and sat down to eat.

"This is delicious! I'll have to invite you to my place to reciprocate."

"I've errands to run in the morning and need to work on Sunday, but tomorrow evening should work."

"Great! I have errands also, so that works well. If you've time, there's an exhibit at the Rubin Museum I'd like to see. We could meet for lunch—there're a lot of wonderful restaurants nearby. Then, after seeing the Rubin, we could go to my place for dinner."

"OK. That should work."

"What work do you have on Sunday?"

"My old job is calling me back. A dear friend has asked me to review the screen edits for a Hollywood musical, and I hate editing musicals. But I'm needed to give guidance on what might be cut to tighten the storyline."

"Sounds interesting."

"I shouldn't complain. I'm sure it'll be fun, but it distracts from my studies."

"Hopefully, it pays well."

"Spoken like an economist!"

As a voting member of the Academy of Motion Picture Arts and Sciences, Sue had obtained a DVD of *Wall Street*. Hank's job was to provide all the financial guidance about the movie while Sue and he watched it. They got through about half the film before they realized the bedroom would be a more appropriate place than the couch for lovemaking.

Over breakfast, they watched the rest of the movie and plotted their day.

"Well, that was probably the most fabulous evening I've ever had last night," Hank said. "Delicious dinner too."

Sue smiled, "Likewise."

"We can meet at the tapas place I mentioned for lunch. Does one p.m. work?"

"Definitely. If I think I'll be late, I'll text you."

"One neat thing about the Rubin is that it never seems to be crowded, and it's always relaxing."

"I've never been, so I'm looking forward to it."

"Cool. Gotta run, but not before saying goodbye." He gave her a big hug and a gentle kiss and was out the door.

Hank reached the tapas place first and found a quiet table at the back.

"So, a New Yorker who hasn't been to the Rubin?" he asked.

"No. It's funny how if you can always visit a place locally, you end up putting it off indefinitely."

"Yes, I've only been twice. They have music events from time to time. I recently went with a friend to hear Meg Okura and her Chamber jazz ensemble. They play jazz with an Asian theme. It was outstanding!"

"I'm sorry I missed it. I've heard Okura perform. Though her training is in classical music, her jazz violin playing defines her. It's extraordinary."

They finished up their tapas and wine and headed over to the Rubin. The special exhibit wasn't exceptional, but Hank enjoyed seeing it and the permanent collection through Sue's eyes. She was much more methodical than he at admiring the artifacts. Hank looked at everything, but often superficially, to get a feel for the museum experience rather than specific works of art. She carefully evaluated select pieces and spent a long time in the Tibetan Shrine room. Afterward, they headed into the gift shop to search for gifts. Hank needed to get more Christmas gifts for his daughters, while Sue wanted to purchase some things for her nephews.

"Thanks for your help on the gifts for my daughters. I never quite know what to get them."

"And thank you for your help! Unfortunately, I still ended up getting them musical things, but hopefully, they'll like them."

After paying, they headed over to Hank's apartment, with its spacious view of the Hudson River, downtown New York skyline, and the Statue of Liberty in the distance. Hank cooked a delicious meal of sole piccata, fried potatoes, asparagus, and his famous dessert—pear wedges *sautéed* in white wine and Cointreau, with cinnamon and lime zest on top. After eating and washing the dishes, they went to the bedroom for more intimacy.

The following day, Sue seemed a little agitated.

"Hank, I need to get back to my place and get to work on this musical."

"No breakfast?"

"No, I often skip it, and the dinner was fantastic last night, so I'm not feeling hungry."

"OK. I'll get in touch later to see how you're doing. And we have Dizzy's to look forward to on Thursday."

She gave him a quick hug and was out the door. Later that day, he emailed her but got no response. She often replied late at night. When on Monday morning he hadn't heard from her, he texted her. Still no response. That evening, he phoned and left a message when she didn't pick up. Finally, she called on Tuesday evening.

"Sue, I'm so glad you phoned. I was getting worried about you. Is everything alright?"

"Yes, I'm fine. But I don't know about us. On Sunday, when I got home, I felt sad and empty. I realized later that I felt ambivalent about our relationship, but don't know why. I'm also not sure about seeing you at Dizzy's this week."

"Wow. I'm sorry to hear that. Sometimes, we feel ambivalent and get over it. So, take your time and let me know. I had a marvelous time on Saturday and Sunday and very much enjoyed your company. Thanks again for the gift suggestions for my daughters. I think they'll like them a lot."

"No problem. Thanks for being understanding."

Hank was in shock. He'd thought all was going well. What had he missed? He'd set it aside for the time being to not think about. It'd work out, or it wouldn't.

On Wednesday evening, Hank met friends at a local bar and had a good time. Life goes on. The more he thought about Sue, the more he realized that their relationship was unlikely to work out. He'd a fun, playful weekend while she felt 'sad and empty.' Such a vast difference of viewpoint on the same weekend didn't bode well for a lasting relationship. When he got home, he was startled to get a call from Sue.

"Hi Hank, I've been thinking, and maybe we could meet at Dizzy's tomorrow."

"Ummm. I just don't get it. Before the weekend, you seemed so positive about me and us. Then, we have what I thought was a lovely weekend together, and you suddenly feel empty about me. What were all the positive comments? A pretense?"

"You sound like you've been drinking."

"Yes, I have. I was out with friends and just got back. And I know that doesn't help with my anger. I'm sorry, but I feel betrayed. And I can't understand what I've done."

"You remember? We talked about anger. We both agreed that we wanted to put those kinds of relationships behind us."

"Yes, I remember."

"I think this ends it for us."

"Yes, I understand."

THE STOLEN BICYCLE

Kemp Hunt walks into his parlor, which he and his wife use as their practice room. Amy is playing the second movement from Tchaikovsky's Violin Concerto and sitting, as usual, near the big bay window. Her long wavy, soft brown hair flows to her bare shoulders, her perfect posture enhancing her beauty. Oddly, the curtains are drawn, and the room is dark, though Kemp sees the sun shining through a crack in the draperies. The high-ceilinged room has flawless acoustics. There are large paintings on the back wall and each side of the door leading to the hallway. Opposite the entrance, just beyond the piano, is an enormous mirror.

They are well-regarded musicians—he a pianist, she a violinist. He sits at the piano to accompany her, pausing to find a good entry point. He launches energetically into the piece, but something is wrong. His hands penetrate the keys, and the piano is silent.

Kemp yells, "What's happening?" Amy does not move. He shouts again, but she doesn't hear him.

He races to the mirror but sees no reflection. With enormous effort, he conjures up a faint trace of his old self—tall, thin, pale with an elegant nose and chin. He's wearing his concert tuxedo. The image fades, and he is exhausted. He sits to recuperate while his wife plays the sad, sonorous melody.

Kemp struggles to recall what transpired in the last few weeks, but his mind is blank. Gradually, he begins remembering past events. He sees himself in bed, dead, a bottle of poison on his bedside table. Yes, he is often depressed. Yes, he contemplates suicide, but he wouldn't do it. Why would he leave Amy? He loves her so much; along with music, she is the joy of his life. His life?

Kemp regards his lifeless body from the ceiling of their bedroom and slowly pulls away. He feels himself drifting upward, experiences itchiness, and then he sees the roof of their house. His wife's car is coming down the drive. But what is that movement in the yard? Someone has stolen his bicycle and is hiding in the bushes. When his wife arrives, the cyclist escapes up the long driveway, unseen by Amy. Kemp follows the cyclist to Adam Wickham's house, where Adam stores the bike in the garage and retires.

Kemp returns home to find his wife weeping at his bedside.

That evening Amy had been in Pittsburgh, performing as the soloist with the local orchestra. But she must have returned earlier than expected, surprising the intruder who needed to escape quickly.

Adam was my golfing buddy!

How could he do this? Memories of Kemp and Adams's outings flooded his mind: Adam's tetchiness when he sliced the ball into the rough; his peevishness when Kemp birdied a hole; his glowing comments on Amy's violin playing and her striking looks.

Kemp's bouts of despair were well-known; the police ruled his death a suicide, and the matter was settled.

This isn't right; I must tell Amy.

Recalling his discomfort when passing through the roof of their house, he walks through Amy; he does it again.

Amy feels a strange coolness. She shudders and resumes playing, but there it is again! She rises and goes to the mirror to check her paleness. While peering into the glass, she sees a faint outline of a person. It's Kemp! How can that be? What is he doing? He's motioning as if he is on a bicycle. Now, he is spelling a word, then he slices his finger across his neck. Amy mouths the word: Adam. Kemp signals a touchdown. Amy's jaw is wide open as the vision fades away.

When had she last seen Kemp's bicycle? He loved his custom-made, light blue touring bike. When Kemp was feeling down, he would go for a long ride and always return refreshed.

Amy looks in their garage and the side of the house where Kemp sometimes placed the bike after a spin but finds nothing. Kemp never lent it to anyone; not even she was allowed to ride it.

Amy phones the police and, with great effort, convinces them to drop by her home. She explains her suspicions but must become distraught before they reluctantly agree to visit Adam.

"Hello, Mr. Wickham," the officer says. "Do you mind if we come in?"

"No," Adam said, motioning the two policemen into his living room. "What can I do for you?"

"Mrs. Hunt seems to think you might know something about a missing bicycle," the second officer says. Adam feigns puzzlement.

Kemp is with them in the living room. He stands in front of the garage doorway, shouting frantically, but to no avail.

How can Kemp get the police to check the garage? He walks over to one officer and tries pushing him in the door's direction but passes through him. He tries again, and again.

"What's in here?" the officer asks Adam.

"That's the garage," Adam replies.

The officer opens the door without asking permission and steps into the darkened space. A light comes on automatically, and he spots the bicycle.

"Oh, yes, I forgot," Adam says. "Kemp lent me his bike before he passed away. Maybe he wanted me to have it?"

In their patrol car, the bike secured in the trunk, the officers phone headquarters to find out who in the area had bought the type of poison that killed Kemp. They return to the Hunt residence and, upon arriving, learn that the purchaser matches Adam's description—medium height, slim, and bald. They drop off the bicycle and return to the Wickham residence.

Kemp is in the parlor with Amy at the exact moment Adam is arrested. He sees a faint smile grace her lips. She picks up her violin and begins to play their favorite duet, Beethoven's *Ode to Joy*. She is saying goodbye.

Kemp regards his tall, graceful wife for a long, languishing moment. But now...now...peace. *Goodbye, my love.*

BOMB THREAT AT BLUES AND BREWS

Jake looked at the ticking time bomb in front of him; he had two choices: red or black, life or oblivion.

It was a beautiful sunny day—perfect for the Blues and Brews Festival held each summer in the bucolic southern Pennsylvania town of Zimmerburg. Jake Fields, head of the security detail for the festival, was touring the site, moving through the throngs of cheerful blues fans. The murmur of the crowd, the music from one of the tents, the colorful clothes of the attendees, and the fragrance of summer sweets from a nearby farm combined to make it a magical day. The festival was in a large field; only a small knoll across the highway broke the flat landscape. The main event of the festival was an hour away, and the air was electric with anticipation.

Security-wise, everything was calm, the people having a good time; no one was even drunk, though that might happen later. Through his walkie-talkie, Jake checked in on his crew of three: Roger, Jim, and Nate. Roger was a character, always signing off "Roger and out." Jim was quiet, never complaining about the long hours or unruly participants.

Nate was hyperactive, always talking, and all over the map when Jake asked how his section of the festival was faring. It wasn't the most professional bunch Jake had worked with, but they got the job done.

Three years earlier, Jake had left the Harrisburg Police department in disgrace. He'd gotten the job despite having shot nerves after returning from Afghanistan, where he defused mines. When he and his partner had confronted a hoodlum on the street, Jake had frozen when the scumbag shot his partner. Fortunately, his partner survived, and the criminal was later apprehended, but Jake was disciplined and could no longer face his colleagues, so he left for this private security job. The pay was OK, but the quality of his coworkers wasn't the same; Jake sometimes needed to step in when they struggled to resolve a confrontation.

Jake's phone rang. It was his wife, Susie.

"What time will you be home tonight?" she asked.

"The festival ends at ten, so I'll be home at about eleven."

"You're busy every weekend. You need to spend time with Jonnie."

"I know. Maybe next week."

"That's what you say every week. Then you play your guitar all week and ignore us."

"Sorry. Can we talk about this later? The main event will start soon."

"It's always something."

"We'll talk tomorrow, OK? I've got to go now," Jake said, and he hung up.

Jake shook his head. But he knew she was right; he hadn't been himself since he let his partner down. His confidence was shaken, and he was terrified he'd freeze in the next emergency he faced. Luckily, nothing much happened in the towns where his security firm operated.

Losing the police job was a big comedown for Jake. He'd returned to his hometown of Harrisburg as a war hero. In Afghanistan, he'd saved many lives with his adroit ability to defuse mines and improvised explosive devices.

"Hello, Jake," the walkie-talkie crackled with a voice Jake recognized but couldn't identify. "Long time no see."

I know that voice, but who the hell is it?

Jake plugged in his earpiece, silencing the walkie-talkie.

"Some guy is listening to us on our walkie-talkies," Jake said into his device as he hastened away from some bystanders. "Put in your earpieces so his voice can't be heard by the crowd." Jake observed Roger across the field of people, wrapping on his earpiece.

"This is Jake Fields. Who am I talking to?"

"I'm the guy that planted a bomb at your festival. A brick of C-4 packed with ball bearings. Enough to kill a whole lot of people. You have forty-eight minutes to find it and defuse it."

Jake checked his watch. The nearest police station was an hour's drive away; he and his team would need to deal with the bomb threat themselves.

What should I do? It could be a hoax.

But Jake had a feeling it wasn't; he knew that voice and sensed the threat was real.

"OK. Roger, Jim, Nate. Listen up. We have to empty the festival field. Do it in a quiet, relaxed manner. Tell them we have a bomb threat, that we don't know how serious it is, but we need to clear the area to be on the safe side. Everyone needs to get to their cars and go home."

"It's serious. Serious enough to wipe out half the crowd," the intruder interjected. "Hey, Roger, Jim, and Nate. Nice to meet you. Don't expect Jake to help you; he's a total fuck-up and always lets his partners down."

Where have I heard that voice?

"Don't pay any attention to him, guys. Just clear the area and keep calm. We're going to get through this."

Jake called the police, who told him they were on their way.

Then it hit Jake—it was Vern Granger, an arsonist he had arrested nine years earlier. Businesses on the verge of bankruptcy would hire him to torch their buildings so they could collect the insurance. Jake caught him climbing out of the window of a commercial property in Harrisburg. The bomb found on the premises had Vern's fingerprints all over it.

Before Jake had met his wife, Susie, Vern had dated her. Jake learned this only after he had been going out with her for a few months; she knew nothing about Vern's line of work. Jake and Susie's love deepened, and they married. Jonnie arrived shortly after that.

After his colleagues had cleared the festival, they all met in the middle of the grounds. Forgetting his walkie-talkie was still on, Jake told his crew that they now had fifteen minutes to find the bomb.

"I'll give you a hint," Vern said. "Jake, you're well equipped to find the explosive. You just need to follow directions to stay alive."

Who does Vern think he is, the Riddler?

"Turn off your walkie-talkies," Jake instructed his squad.

"Do you want me to find the bomb?" Roger asked, his voice quavering.

"I could help," said Nate, putting his shaking hand in the air.

Jim cleared his throat and said, "Well, I guess I could try, if you want me to, Jake."

"Guys, I appreciate your volunteering, but I'm the only one experienced at this. I defused mines in Afghanistan. Now, here is what we're going to do..."

The group spread out and Jake headed toward the main stage where all the sound equipment was located. Vern wanted him to find the bomb, so he switched back on his walkie-talkie.

"Am I getting warm, Vern," Jake asked.

"Oh, so you *do* remember me. You jailed me and took my girl. Now, I'm going to put you down. I guess my clue on equipment was too easy."

"Where in the main stage will I find it?"

"Oh, you wish."

"What?" Jake asked. "You can't come up with any other clever clues?"

"Hmmph. Try this one: You'll need to look for a fallen angel."

Jake entered the backstage area and looked around.

Fallen angel?

Two men were laboring over an overweight teenager on the ground, his leg entangled in a shoddily built staircase.

"You need to leave the area. Now!" Jake said to them.

"It's not a hoax?" One of them asked.

"No, this is real. Get out of here!"

"Will you take care of our buddy, Clive? He broke his ankle, and it's stuck in this staircase," the other said. Then they ran away.

"Help me," Clive said. "I can't move."

"Stay calm. Everything's going to be alright."

"Am I going to die?" Clive said, his face flushed and pinched.

"Not if I can help it. But I could use that wire cutter on your hip," Jake said, after spying the clippers on the kid's leather utility belt.

"Take 'em." Clive pulled the tool off his waist and handed it to Jake.

Jake looked behind the speakers, under the sound control panel and the stage. Toward the back of the stage there was a miscellaneous pile of equipment, junk it would seem.

Then he saw it—a cheap imitation of a Tom Anderson Angel Player guitar with a couple of broken strings. He lifted it up and saw the bomb.

"You have sixty seconds, Jake. Are you going to run, or take your chances?"

Jake quickly cleared the other things away from the device and pulled out the clippers.

"Thirty seconds."

Don't freeze!

There were two wires activating the detonator, which was attached to a digital timer; but only one wire would stop it from exploding. The red one had a tag on it: "Cut me and save your life."

Follow directions to stay alive, Vern had said.

"Ten seconds, Jake. Then, kaboom!" Vern cackled.

Make a decision!

Jake cut the black cord, and the timer stopped. Jake let out a sigh of relief, wiped his brow, turned off his walkie-talkie, and telephoned Jim with his cell phone.

"Jim, you can close in on him now. The bomb's defused."
Earlier, Jake had told his team to surround Vern on the knoll
above the festival grounds and wait for his instructions. Jake
knew that the hill was the only vantage point to observe the
festival and had a hunch Vern would be there, watching him
instead of his crew.

With guns drawn, Jim, Roger, and Nate handcuffed Vern
and waited for the police to arrive. Jake phoned the ambulance that was still waiting nearby and sat with Clive until the
medics appeared. Later, he watched as the cops shoved Vern,
swearing obscenities, into a police car.

The following weekend, the local paper had a feature on Jake
and how he saved everyone at the festival, including Clive,
and the festival's equipment. The organizers stayed an extra
day to present the last event, which went off without a hitch.
Susie read the news story aloud to Jake and Jonnie as they
ate breakfast. Jake was embarrassed but pleased his wife was
proud of him. Of course, he had earlier suffered a severe
scolding for attempting to tackle the bomb.

"So, you're a hero, Dad?"

"Not really. It was just something I had to do," Jake said.
"Sometimes scary things happen during my work, but
not often."

"You'll be OK?" Jonnie asked.

"Sure. I can take care of myself. Hey, how about we go to
the ball game today? The local team is playing its rival."

"That would be great! I'll take my glove in case a ball comes
our way."

"Good idea. You can keep us safe from stray fouls."

As they headed out the door for the ballpark, Jake said, "Hey, Jonnie, did I ever tell you about the time I caught an arsonist?"

Susie watched them from the window as they got into the car, a smile on her face.

THE SPIRIT CLUB

G rant entered Jeffrey's house, carefully wiping his feet on the *"Welcome"* mat decorated with ghouls and goblins. He was the first to arrive, followed shortly by the other widowers—Barrett, Avery, and Elbert. They each meticulously wiped their shoes on the doormat upon arrival.

Grant had lost his wife, Emily, in a car accident the year before, and his behavior had changed. The other day, he had snapped at a store clerk who had shorted him a farthing. What did it matter? He moped at home and seldom got out; these monthly meetings with his four friends were about all he did socially. Having lost his own wife, Jeffrey helped Grant with his grieving process after his loss. They had become the closest of friends. Still, Grant could not help resenting life and the living. What was the point without Emily?

Jeffrey's home was a classic row house in Tufnell Park. The group always gathered in the dark walnut walled drawing room just off the hallway entrance. The curtains were drawn, and the room was lit by a low-wattage chandelier. One corner held a small desk, another the liquor cabinet. But the key fixture of the room was the large round table with five evenly spaced chairs placed immediately below the lighting. Each of the members secretly hoped to reconnect with their wives, but that had not happened so far.

Jeffrey waited until all four guests arrived and then handed each of them a whiskey tumbler before raising his own glass for a toast.

"May the phantoms from above and beyond join our Spirit Club this evening. Welcome!"

"Welcome!" the other four members of the club echoed, downing the drink in one quaff.

As they were sitting down, Elbert remarked, "I thought we had a wonderful spirit visit us last month. I'm so glad I could conjure up Mrs. Heath to explain how her husband murdered her. Utterly delightful."

"You didn't bring her to us," Grant said. "I did."

"Elbert. Grant. Please," Jeffrey said. "I'm sure we all helped to fetch Mrs. H. And we can do the same tonight, I hope."

"Hear, hear," the four fellows confirmed.

"Shall we?" Jeffrey asked, gesturing at the table. They all sat down in their preferred chairs. "Hands down, gentlemen." With their hands on the table, palms down, they closed their eyes.

"Spirits of the underworld come and join us—welcome!" they chanted, repeating the phrase over and over, pausing to listen after each mantra. Minutes passed. An hour passed. The incantation continued.

"I feel a presence," Grant said. "But I'm not sure we should bring it in. It's cold and dark."

"I sense evil!" Elbert said.

"Turn it away, Grant!" Avery said.

"Don't let it in!" Jeffrey said.

"I...I...I'm not sure I can stop it," Grant said.

The curtains swayed, they felt a chilly breeze, and heard fierce scraping at the welcome mat.

"What are you?" Elbert screamed, and they all opened their eyes to see him stand and jump backward, his chair tumbling beneath him. Elbert's eyes were opened so wide, Grant thought they might pop out. His body was shaking, and his hair frizzed out as if he were receiving an electric shock. They all leaped up, knocking over their chairs as they gaped at Elbert.

Elbert, struggling to stay upright, was flung across the room to the far wall. A painting fell as he slammed against it. Something braced him there for a long moment, while the others continued to stare. Then the shuddering stopped, and he stood erect, walking toward his friends, stopping about five feet away.

A deep, gravelly groan came from Elbert's mouth. "*I AM EREBUS, GOD OF DARKNESS, AND I AM HERE TO DEVOUR YOU SELFISH, PETTY BEINGS. I'LL START WITH THIS WORTHLESS SOUL.*"

Grant glanced over at the shredded doormat, which was now partially visible in the vestibule. When he looked back at Elbert, his shape was morphing, growing larger. All his skin was being stretched out and was rippling as if snakes were beneath the surface, pushing to escape the confines of his body. Then he heard a loud slurping sound and watched Elbert's scalp disappear. Then, his eyes were gone, sucked into the evil being. What was left of Elbert was still standing, but now he had no head, and his shoulders were being eaten away, while the skin continued to writhe. The loud smacking sound of a giant tongue licking its chops came from his disappearing corpse. The stench of rotten intestines filled the air, gagging the four observers who stood frozen next to their toppled chairs. Elbert's torso was now gone, but his two legs remained upright, slowly being gobbled up by Erebus. Eventually, there was nothing left but a puddle of brownish liquid.

The four remaining friends looked around the room and at each other. Was the creature gone? The room was so quiet they could hear the grandfather clock ticking like a beating drum.

"AND NOW FOR MY NEXT VICTIM."

"Agh!" Jeffrey said as Erebus pitched him to the wall.

"Not Jeffrey!" Grant said, leaping forward and grabbing his hand. Grant's mind flooded with memories of Jeffrey coaching him on how to act at work, helping him to paint his house, and comforting him after his wife died. He grabbed Jeffrey's hand, even as the vile spirit consumed him from top to bottom. Jeffrey's eyes popped back into his head as Erebus glugged them down. Grant's efforts seem to slow the monster, but it wasn't enough, and Jeffrey was soon reduced to a pool of gooey fluid. Grant's hand was holding Jeffrey's hand, all that was left of him. He dropped it to the floor, staring at Jeffrey's final remains. But he thought he had sensed a weakness in the ghoul.

"YOU'RE NEXT," Erebus intoned, directing his disembodied voice toward Grant.

"Quick!" Grant said to his two remaining mates. "Hold my hands!"

Grant grabbed Avery with his left hand and Barrett with his right and continued, "Repeat after me: 'Erebus, out! Evil, out!'"

The three of them chanted the phrase over and over, their hands locked in a tight embrace, eyes squeezed shut. Grant thought momentarily about the adequacy of their chant but concluded it didn't matter; they just needed to bellow together. Over and over. As one.

First, Erebus tested Grant. Grant felt an enormous pressure on his chest, as if someone were standing on him, though he was upright. But he continued to repeat their new mantra, and the heaviness eased. Next, Avery was quivering under the strain of Erebus's efforts to enter him. Grant held him tight, and Avery's quaking diminished. Finally, the foul shadow attacked Barrett again and again, but Barrett never stopped shouting for Erebus to leave. Despite the shuddering house, falling paintings, smashed glasses, and the stench of rotten flesh, they held hands and screamed together.

Finally, dawn broke, sending a sliver of sunshine through a crack in the curtains.

Slowly, they opened their eyes and surveyed the room. The brackish puddles were gone, the room a mess, but calm. They had vanquished Erebus.

A few months later, Avery, Barrett, and Grant met in Avery's parlor for their monthly book club. Two other friends and recent widowers, Martin and Albert, joined them. Avery served everyone tea and left a fresh pot on his tea table. They all settled into their places on the sofa and the easy chairs.

"First, we'll discuss our book of the month, *The Three Musketeers*," Avery said. "Then Grant has a suggestion to make."

The five friends discussed the classic novel with great animation and many gesticulations. It was like a tennis match with Avery, Barrett, Martin and Albert praising the intrigue, the duels, the trysts, and the amorous interludes. Grant, alone in opposition, parried with phrases such as "overwrought," "weakly motivated characters," "ridiculous plot twists," and "frivolous love affairs." But his efforts were not enough to overcome the onslaught of volleys, and the four friends won the match, crushing Grant.

"Well, I think we've settled that!" Avery said, a huge grin on his face. "Grant, you may now raise your proposal for discussion."

"Thank you, Avery," Grant said. "Yes, I think we should resurrect our seances. We're five members again, and that's an ideal number to reach into the beyond. I know we had a stressful final session, but we had many remarkable encounters before that one."

"But Elbert and Jeffrey disappeared!" Martin said. "The police couldn't find a trace of them."

"Yes, I know," said Grant. "But I'm sure they're in a better place now."

"God rest their souls," Avery said.

"Amen," replied the others.

"I also feel we could use a little more excitement in our lives," Barrett said. "I'd do it again."

"You're crazy," Albert said. "But I'll try it if you think it can be safe."

"Three of us survived," Avery said. "And anyway—what have we got to lose?"

Barrett said, "Avery, do you remember Mrs. Heath? She was so entertaining!"

"Yes," Avery said, "and who knows? Maybe we'll be able to reconnect to one of our wives."

"We did have some very interesting guests visit us," said Grant, a glint of satisfaction in his eye as he recalled their last visitor.

DEATH BY GUNSHOT

Colin Burrows began his summer job as a bookmobile librarian in Zimmerburg, a bucolic town in southern Pennsylvania, in June 2019. He had hoped for a better internship, but this was all he could find. He worried that a degree in English Literature might not lead to financial security. Colin couldn't graduate from college with a low-paying career, disappointing his mother. They had struggled emotionally and financially after his dad killed himself when Colin was eleven; he'd need to take more programming classes to capitalize on his geeky computer skills.

His predecessor at the bookmobile, Nicole Cress, had died recently, under unusual circumstances; a gunshot to her right temple was ruled a suicide by the police. On his first day of work, Colin noticed that nobody had cleaned out Nicole's things from the bookmobile. In the glove compartment, he found her bank book showing $70,126 in her account and a photo of two women, one of whom a colleague identified as Nicole. These personal effects sparked his inquisitiveness; who was this mysterious Nicole?

Colin's job was straightforward; he drove the bookmobile to all corners of the county each week, delivering books and accounting for all the borrowings on his computer.

The bookmobile was cool; its sides were emblazoned with *"Library On Wheels"* and a giant picture book; the back had an idyllic interior scene with a woman reading to a group of children. Fortunately, Colin was not expected to do this; he doubted he would be good with kids. But Nicole had enthralled the community's offspring for twenty years with her inspired reading of stories. The interior was lined with books that the library members could browse; a door led to the driver's area. A fan that made an odd flapping sound was in the middle of the truck's roof. Colin had to stoop his tall, lean frame when standing in the back; his mop of light brown curly hair often brushed the ceiling.

Colin's work left him plenty of time to investigate Nicole. On his computer, he quickly unearthed her birth date, August 2, 1948, in Orient, Iowa, and a photo from her high school yearbook. But the snapshot looked nothing like either of the two women in the picture he'd found in the glove box. His spare time was now spent searching for more information about Nicole. Why had she committed suicide?

He made a startling discovery: Nicole Cress died in 1994; he found her obituary in the local paper archives of Des Moines, Iowa; the photo matched the one in the yearbook. The date and place of birth were the same as the Zimmerburg Nicole, whom he began to call Nico. But Orient, Iowa, had less than a thousand people; there couldn't be two Nicole Cresses, let alone two born on the same day. Nicole had died four years before Nico arrived in Zimmerburg. Who was Nico?

One day, while tidying the books on the shelves, Colin discovered a hidden bundle of letters tied with a string. He read a few of them; they were endearing letters between two sisters.

The envelopes had Nicole's name and address on them, but the letters all began with "Dear Agnes." The envelope's return address was from Lois Rose in Tucson, Arizona. The postmarks began in 1998 when Nico arrived in Zimmerburg.

The following day, after dispensing with the customers, Colin researched Lois Rose in Tucson and discovered an article about her sister Agnes. Agnes had married John Franklin, an attorney in Tucson, but he had tragically died in 1996. The article implied John was having an affair with another attorney in town, but the police declared the death a suicide and cleared Agnes of wrongdoing. To Colin, that still did not explain the furtive journey of Agnes Rose to Zimmerburg, but he had run out of leads and stopped researching. He wrote to Lois, informing her of Agnes's death; he felt obligated to those left behind by a loved one. Lois wrote back, thanking him for his condolences. He also informed Lois of Agnes's bank account, she could collect the money as the sole survivor.

One day in July, Colin pulled the bookmobile into a small town and parked in front of the Post Office as usual. After Colin finished with his clientele, the Postmaster gave him a letter addressed to the "Bookmobile Librarian." Colin opened the envelope; it was a ransom note with words clipped out of magazines! The letter, addressed to A. Franklin, said the writer had been on the street outside her house the night of her husband's death, heard a shot, peered in the window, and saw Agnes holding a gun while standing over her husband. The witness had seen Agnes wipe the gun clean of fingerprints and place it in her husband's hand. Agnes was to meet the blackmailer at the quarry outside of Zimmerburg on April 15, 2019, and bring $50,000 in cash, half of Agnes's life insurance payment after her husband's death. The envelope was postmarked April 11 from a nearby town. The letter was three months late, and Agnes would have missed the rendezvous at the quarry.

Colin searched the bookmobile methodically. Then, remembering the funny noise from the fan vent, he took off its grill. Inside were two letters, one from 1996, the other from the week before Agnes killed herself. They both had the same content as the letter he received from the Postmaster; the blackmailer had traced Agnes to Zimmerburg, just like Colin had.

Colin paced back and forth in the bookmobile. *Why did Agnes kill herself?*

Was it because the blackmailer had found her? But why not pay him off? Surely that would be easier than suicide?

Colin jumped on his computer and reread the story of her husband's death. He died of a bullet to the right temple, precisely how Agnes had ended her life.

Colin emitted a long sigh, shut down his computer, and steered the bookmobile to his favorite bar in Zimmerburg. Agnes had shot herself out of remorse for killing her husband.

THE TREE TALKER

Myra leaps out of bed at six and makes herself a cup of tea, pouring in a small splash of soy milk. Then she rushes out to greet her old friend, Birks. As she is hugging Birks, Chad passes by on his morning walkabout of the donut-shaped space station DaphneX, where they live. DaphneX is one of many stations circling Earth. Each biosphere has its own climate to preserve a specific set of animal and plant species now that the Earth is too hot to inhabit. On DaphneX, technology is kept to a minimum except for AIGU, the AI computer that regulates everything. The citizens prefer to be close to nature.

Birks greets Myra with a warm good morning, describing all the facets of his well-being. Myra replies in kind.

"Talking to your tree friend, Myra?" Chad teases. Myra ignores him.

No one on the station believes she communicates with plants. It's not talking, but Myra opens her mind and her heart to sense their thoughts and feel their concerns. Birks, a giant fifty-year-old birch tree, is only ten years older than Myra, but he seems much wiser to her. Underground networks connect Birks to all the other birch trees on DaphneX, so communing with Birks is like talking to a family.

As Chief Biologist, Myra and her staff manage the health of all the vegetation on DaphneX. She discovered her gift for tree talking when she was twelve and fell out of a tree, breaking her arm. When she propped herself against the tree, she felt its sympathy. Ever since then, she'd been able to speak to trees, but was terrified of climbing them. The fall may have also stunted her growth. At four feet ten inches, Myra was, as she liked to say, "efficient."

Each day, after a brief meeting, Myra and her staff tour a part of DaphneX. The citizens have well-established passageways to follow, minimizing any harm to the plants and animals. Occasionally, they stop and exam a tree or plant to discuss its health. When they do this, Myra always holds a leaf or branch, communing with the organism. However, she never mentions to her team what she feels from the plant; her team needs to decide its health independently.

DaphneX is filled with lush green trees and plants. Sometimes, the team spots a squirrel or mole racing across the path. The bees and butterflies are out in full force, flitting among the flowers that line the trail. The earthy smells of healthy plants and the sweetness of flowers fill their nostrils. A mild artificial breeze from giant fans rustles the hair on their necks. The spinning of DaphneX creates gravity for them along the outermost edge of the donut. Myra looks up to see the tops of the trees and just beyond them the thin tube that houses AIGU and runs along the inner circle of the space station.

After their excursion, Myra returns to her compound to relax. Following a leisurely lunch, she gives Birks a quick squeeze but jumps back, her face flush with anguish.

Birks is not well. Myra hears other plants crying. She embraces Birks and listens. Birks tells Myra about the nutrients they are receiving; they believe poison has been added and it will kill them by morning. There is only one explanation: AIGU is poisoning the plants.

What has gone wrong? The plants sustain the humans on DaphneX and harming them should be against AIGU's core principles. Its learning algorithm must have taken a dark turn. But how? In the centuries of AIGU's existence, was a malicious path inevitable at some point?

Myra listens to Birks while he provides her with an idea of how to solve the problem. Myra, eyes closed, and ear pressed to the tree trunk, begins to cry, the tears flooding down her cheeks. She jumps back, shaking her head furiously. "There must be another way!"

Myra runs into her hut and springs in front of her computer; her fingers fly across the keys as she questions it again and again. The answer is always the same, and Birks has already told her what needs to be done. Myra pounds her desk with her fists.

"Myra! Quick!" Chad shouts, rushing into Myra's hut. "The plants are dying!"

"I know," Myra says in a quiet voice, wiping her tears away and turning to Chad. "Birks told me."

"You and your talking plants—this is an emergency! We'll all die if the plants go!"

"Chad, this is what you need to do." Myra, her face calm, quickly gives him instructions. Then she goes into her lab and mixes a variety of chemicals with natural herbs derived from the station's plant life.

AIGU is self-contained, auto-repairing and lives above them on the inner core of the circular station. The only way to reprogram it is by going through one of two hoops at the end of the AIGU's tube. These are directly above Myra's compound. However, AIGU has never needed a software patch, so the citizens long ago repurposed the mechanical cranes that were used to reach it. And, in keeping with the citizens' wishes, there are no flying ships on DaphneX.

Her mixture complete, Myra fills bucket after bucket with it and water, then pours the concoction on Birks's roots. Birks grows.

Chad runs up to Myra as she is pouring the last bucket at Birks's base. "I've got it," he says, holding up the memory card she had asked him to prepare. "How are we going to get it up, through the hoop, and into AIGU?"

"Birks will be tall enough soon for someone to climb up and enter AIGU's home."

"How did you do that?" Chad asks.

"Chemicals," Myra says, shaking her head. "There's no time to explain."

"OK. I'll go up Birks." Chad says. "You don't climb trees."

"Birks's upper branches are too fragile for someone of your weight. I'll have to go."

"Myra. Are you sure?"

"No, I'm not!"

By this time, a large crowd has gathered, all concerned about the plants on whom they depend. Myra, the smallest adult amongst them, surveys their pale faces and watches as they wring their hands. An eerie moan emanates from the surrounding flora as the trees agitate from an unseen breeze.

What to do?

Myra's stomach is in knots, coiled tight as she pockets the memory stick. She walks over to Birks, looks up and swoons, staggering backward—Birks is so tall! She recovers and, using a leather strap wrapped around Birks, Myra tries to shinny up his trunk. But she's never done this before. She tries again. And again. Gradually, she gets the hang of it and reaches the lower branches. She secures the strap around her waist, then looks down. Big mistake. A wave of vertigo overcomes her, but she holds Birks tightly.

Myra senses Birks directing her ascent from branch to branch. She just needs to feel Birks's guidance.

When she is level with the hoop, she stretches out her hand to grasp it, but it's too far away. The hoop is a foot wide and ten feet tall, like a giant earring.

Between her legs, she feels Birks sway. Myra rocks back and forth, back and forth, until she can leap from the tree to the hoop. Myra jumps, grabs the hoop, but its curved edges are slippery. She scrambles for a better grip, slips, then does a quick pull-up, grasping more of the hoop. With that embrace, she swings her right leg through the hoop and flips herself into the tube that houses AIGU.

Following Chad's directions, she inserts the computer card into AIGU.

Returning to the hoop, she leaps to Birks, who catches her. The descent is easier.

The following morning, Myra crawls out of bed. Chad's computer patch solved the fertilizer problem. He had simply copied the code which instructs AIGU to protect humans and replaced "human" with "plants and animals." With this added to its ethics, AIGU is protecting all organisms.

Myra walks out to say good morning to Birks, who is dying. Birks had known the growth fertilizer would kill him, but he and Myra realized it was the only way to get into AIGU in time to save DaphneX. A steady stream of tears flows from Myra's eyes, but she isn't sobbing or sniffling. A calmness overwhelms her.

Myra hugs Birks for the last time, feeling love and goodness flow between them.

BETRAYAL AT THE AUTO SHOW

N*ever try to outdrink a Russian.*
Craig dragged himself out of bed and made his way to the espresso machine, his head throbbing. He'd done OK: he found out the Russians also knew about a major betrayal taking place at the Jacob Javits auto show. But, while Craig's chess playing rapidly deteriorated with each shot of vodka, Oleg's skills seemed only to improve. Today, he had to outfox Oleg and didn't feel remotely up to it.

A fellow spy was going to hand over some weapon technology to the Chinese for a million dollars. The setup made little sense. His colleague, whoever he was, had tipped off his own team that he was betraying his country, and he'd also told the Russians. Maybe he really didn't want to give the secrets to the Chinese, but thought he could collect the money? He hoped Oleg and Viktor would fight with Craig and his partner, Andy, while he made his escape?

Anyway, the bureau chief didn't want to call in the police unless the memory stick holding the information was at risk of leaving the country. It would be too embarrassing if the agency were to have a mole arrested while giving away state secrets. So, the chief assigned Craig and Andy to retrieve the flash drive, identify the mole, and escape the scene without being detected. *A cakewalk: we'll nab the mole, take the stick from the Chinese agent, thank them, and walk away. Why would they resist?*

Craig arrived at Jacob Javits just as the show was opening. The man at the door scanned his QR code on his phone and Craig walked into the cavernous showroom filled with a zillion cars and people.

While surveying the convention hall, Craig got a text from Andy. Someone had slammed into his car and the police had arrived immediately. He'd be late. *Great. Should make this job even easier.*

This would be a transfer of a small thing for a big parcel. The Chinese would probably use one of their agents to pick up the stick—they presumably didn't know his bureau and the Russians had been tipped off. Craig searched the crowd for a Chinese man carrying a heavy bag; a million bucks in hundred-dollar bills was twenty-two pounds.

Craig spotted Oleg and Viktor almost immediately. Both were doing the same thing he was: scanning the room. They looked a little smug, so Craig assumed they'd arranged for Andy's accident.

Craig spied the Chinese agent next. He had an army-green duffle bag slung over his shoulder, and he was wearing a red bandanna around his neck.

This is too easy.

It was.

There was another Chinese man with an identical bag and a blue kerchief. And another with a white one. *Red, white, and blue. Cute.*

Then Craig spotted a character with a white bandanna. He wore a mask and under his baseball cap he sported a cheap wig. He was walking toward the Asian with the white neck scarf. Glancing around quickly, Craig saw the other two handover people, both in the same ridiculous disguise, but with red and blue scarves. Craig had a one-in-three chance of being right—just like that shell game played on the sidewalk.

Red: too obvious. White: too boring.

The disguised person with the blue kerchief thrust the memory stick into the Chinese's hand, ripped the bag off his shoulder, and dashed away. Craig lunged at the Chinese guy, who seemed paralyzed with shock at the abrupt exchange. Craig now had the drive in his hand, but the Chinese gentleman recovered and pummeled him with a flurry of blows.

Shit! This guy knows karate!

Craig was suddenly on the floor, suffering from accurately place blows to his back and head. He wrapped his legs around the one of the Chinese's legs and rolled over quickly, bringing the man down. A sharp elbow to the head knocked him out.

But Oleg and Viktor were converging on Craig.

Where is Andy?

Craig jumped up and started running toward the exit where he had entered. He thrust his hand with the stick into his right jacket pocket, pulled it out, and sprinted. Craig dashed around one car, then another. He jumped onto the hood of an auto to slide across, avoiding a gaggle of ogling people.

Viktor was gaining on him, but Craig made it to the exit before feeling someone grab his jacket. Craig slammed into the ticket guy, sending his scanner spinning across the floor.

He saw Andy in the distance and was about to wave and shout when everything went black.

Craig awoke from a heavily sedated slumber. Two Andys swum into his vision before gradually merging into one.

"Where am I?" Craig asked.

"The hospital. The Russians sandbagged you at Javits. Remember anything?"

"Oh, yeah. The memory stick and cash transfer. They looked like cartoon characters."

"The boss is going to be furious with you. We were supposed to bring in the police if we couldn't handle it. Not get arrested by them for knocking over a ticket collector. The Russians got your jacket and escaped before I could catch them. Stupidly, I stayed to help my stricken partner."

"Thanks, pal."

"Tell me the flash drive wasn't in it."

"I had a memory stick in my jacket. It held detailed information about a high-tech toilet. This should be the real one." Craig stuck out his right arm and ejected a drive from a gadget on his right wrist. "Check it out."

Andy opened his computer on the bed, fired it up, and inserted the stick in the side. "Holy shit. This is weapon information! Not bad. Too bad we couldn't catch our mole."

"I got a good look at the guy making the transfer. It was Jason from our tech department."

Andy whistled. "You've still got it, bro'." They fist pumped.

"Yes. Oleg may be better at chess than I am, but I'm better at shell games and sleights of hand."

THE DEUCE OF CLUBS

D amian watched the animations of his boss, Clay Brewer, as if viewing a Saturday morning cartoon. Clay's excited gesticulations were creating the image of a tornado around his head.

"I smell a rat!" Clay said. "This lady sued our client too quickly after her husband's death. How could she come up with that? She's supposed to be grieving! And we're on the hook for the life insurance policy, which her husband just took out!" Sweat glistened on the top of Clay's bald head, while his jowls jiggled like Jell-O.

Damian was dressed in his usual light gray suit, white shirt, and pencil-thin black tie. He couldn't look more different from Clay. Clay was large, flabby, and bald. Damian was short, with gym-hardened muscles, and a crew cut, the same hairstyle he'd had in the Marines.

Damian reviewed the case in his mind while his boss ranted. The facts were straightforward according to the police report and from what he had seen of the room where Baz Hodges had died. Damian, a former cop, had been allowed to view the scene after the police had completed their investigation. It wasn't pretty. Baz was in a chair, his head thrown back, his mouth agape, a large bloodstain on his shirt where the bullet had entered his chest, killing him instantly. Baz was a big bruiser of a redhead, now overweight, but still with huge biceps. A single playing card, the two of clubs, was on the table in front of him; the rest of his cards were spread around his feet. Other cards, Chinese takeout boxes, and chopsticks were strewn on the kitchen floor. Baz, Darren Brown, Forrest Keller, and Vernon Douglas had been playing poker at Forrest's place. Forrest had dropped his gun, for which he had a legal permit, and it had discharged, sending a bullet through Baz's heart. The hole in the table confirmed that the gunshot came from the floor. Forrest claimed it was an accident and Darren and Vern had backed him up. In surveying the room, Damian had seen nothing to dispute the police report. The report also documented how distraught both Forrest and Mrs. Hodges were by Baz's death.

Mrs. Sally Hodges was due to collect $500,000 on Baz's life insurance policy. Now, she was suing Forrest, also a Raxalan Insurance Company client, for another half million. According to Sally, Forrest was negligent; he should have secured all guns before starting the poker game.

"Baz is dead," Damian said. "That's clear."

"I know, and I'm sorry about that," Clay said. "If it's legitimately an accident, we'll pay the claim. But if it's fraud, we won't pay."

"Are you suggesting that Baz was murdered? If so, you're reaching a different conclusion from the police."

"Something's fishy. It all seems too well planned: the financial stress of the Hodges, the recent procurement of a life insurance policy, the rapidity of the negligence suit. Find out what really happened. I'll stall on the life claim, and we'll initiate legal proceedings over the liability claim."

"Yes, sir. I'm on it."

Damian talked to Darren and Vern, both of whom reiterated their story that Forrest's gun had gone off accidentally. The only new thing he learned was that Forrest was furious about being sued for negligence by Sally. He believed, rightly, that his home insurance policy was likely to be more expensive in the future. Damian visited Forrest next.

"Mr. Keller, was there any reason you needed a gun at the poker game?" Damian asked after Forrest had invited him into his living room and served him a coffee.

"It was a new gun, and I wanted to show it to my friends," Forrest replied. "Tragically, when I pulled it out, I dropped it and it fired off a round, killing Baz. Vern, Darren, Baz, and I have been friends since high school. We play poker once a week and watch the Eagles' games together. You can't imagine how awful I feel."

Damian could hear the stress in Forrest's voice, but something wasn't quite right. He couldn't put his finger on it; was it a tinge of triumph? He thanked Forrest for his time and stepped out into a sunny fall day in South Philadelphia. The leaves in the trees planted along the street rustled in the breeze. The air was fresh, and he could smell cheesesteaks being cooked in a nearby café. He turned and started walking toward his car.

"Pssst," someone said from the porch of the house next to Forrest's home.

Damian checked Forrest's windows; no one was watching him, so he mounted the steps and introduced himself.

"Come in," his newfound friend said. "I'm Todd Wells, and I've known Forrest, Darren, Vern, and Baz since we were teenagers. I don't know why the police didn't interview me."

"What would you have told them if they did?"

"Forrest always hated Baz, who was a bully in school; he picked on everybody, but Forrest got the worst of it. Even Darren and Vern got beat up from time to time, but Forrest was Baz's regular punching bag. Forrest also told me they all suspected Baz cheated at cards, but they were afraid to challenge him."

"So, you think it wasn't an accident?"

"No way. A guy drops a gun, it goes off, and shoots a guy in the heart? Doesn't sound likely to me!"

"But Vern and Darren have backed up Forrest's story."

"Saving their friend from jail? Sure, I would too; wouldn't you?"

"Thanks for your time, Mr. Wells," Damian said. "Can I talk to you again if I have further questions?" They traded phone numbers, and Damian walked to his car, mulling over this new information.

Maybe his boss was right? Could Forrest have bent over to tie his shoe and plugged Baz from under the table? Friendships in South Philly were strong, that was certain; with Baz dead, Forrest's friends might just stick with him, rather than rat him to the police.

Damian headed over to the police headquarters to review the files on all the suspects. He found startling information in the files, which he'd follow up on later. However, he needed to meet with Sally first. He'd arranged a meeting for late afternoon, and he made it just in time. Because she had filed a negligence claim against their client Forrest, both their lawyers were present.

"Thank you for agreeing to meet with us, Mrs. Hodges," Damian said. "We hope to resolve this matter without going to court."

"Pay the claim and we won't need to go to court," Sally retorted. "Forrest shouldn't have had a weapon at a poker game. My husband is dead because of Forrest's negligence." She sniffled and wiped a tissue at her eye, but Damian couldn't see a tear.

"Isn't it true, Mrs. Hodges, that your husband brutally beat you and you filed police reports on him on three separate occasions before dropping the charges?"

"You don't have to answer that!" Sally's lawyer said, but Damian could see the color draining from her face and her eyes flaring.

"Your neighbors have interesting stories about the fights you and Baz had. Sometimes they complained about the noise." Damian was guessing on this one, but South Philly row houses weren't known for their sound insulation. "You know, Forrest isn't happy about your liability claim against him; he told me it was your idea for him to shoot your husband."

"That dirty son-of-a-bitch! I was going to give him and his buddies some of the life insurance..." Sally stopped in mid-sentence, realizing her mistake.

"Yes, I think the police might be interested in your arrangement with Forrest, Darren, and Vern," Damian said.

Sally's lawyer had turned white as a sheet and moved as far away from Sally as he could. Raxalan's attorney was sporting a Mona Lisa smile: enigmatic.

"Great job, Damian," Clay said.

"Yep," Damian said, "I solved this murder case, which means Raxalan is off the hook for the life insurance and the liability claim. Does this mean I get a bonus this year?"

"Sure. I'll get you a giant turkey for Thanksgiving."

"Thanks, boss," Damian said so drily that you could hear the splitting of wood in a kiln.

THE PACKAGE

Rolf's throat tightened as he listened to his boss explain the mission.

"This is a delicate operation; the package is fragile and expensive," Thomas, his boss, said in a slightly higher-pitched tone than usual. "The client has given us strict orders to be absolutely discreet; not even the police are to be contacted should you encounter any difficulties, not that we expect any. You are to complete this assignment alone. Of course, I chose you because you are our best agent. Any questions?"

"No," Rolf said. "It's straightforward. I contact someone, name unknown, on a secure telephone. He gives me a place and meeting time to be handed a key to a locker in the train section of the Zurich Airport. I retrieve the contents from the locker and deliver it to Wolfgang von Rothenburg, the director of the Geneva Gem Show. But why can't the person with the key just give me the goods?"

"I'm not absolutely sure, but I gather it has something to do with the security of the person who owns the merchandise and the secrecy of the mission. Only we know it is valuable. They have your photo, so will spot you at the meeting place."

Rolf Weiss left the office of Kunst Security Services, a firm specializing in the protection and transport of art and returned to his apartment in Zurich. Rolf was medium-height, extremely fit and agile, balding with pale blue eyes. He was used to working unaided and to secrecy, but this mission made his chest tighten. Something didn't feel right; Thomas was not easily ruffled.

Rolf opened his large art deco wardrobe. His suits were perfectly aligned. His shirts, all white and lightly starched, were also neatly arrayed. He opened the top drawer of the built-in bureau and selected a burner phone from the evenly spaced row of them in front of him.

At 3:00 p.m., Rolf phoned the designated number and was told to meet in one hour at the Max Bill Pavilion sculpture just off Bahnhofstrasse. It's like a miniature Stonehenge, but the gray granite rectangular columns are all at right angles. After arriving, he sat on one of the prone pillars and was soon approached by a gentleman who nodded at him and gave him an envelope.

"This seems too easy," Rolf thought.

To retrieve the parcel, Rolf just needed to get to the airport, so he walked the short distance to the Hauptbahnhof and caught the next train there. As usual, the train was on schedule and arrived precisely at the designated time. He disembarked, took the escalator to the station area, and walked toward the lockers.

As he approached them, he noticed someone look at him and signal through a microphone on his lapel to two other men, who both jerked their heads up to view him. They recognized him! He was about a hundred yards from them, so he turned and ran back to the escalators. Glancing at the departure board, he saw a train was leaving in one minute.

He flew down the stairway and leapt onto the train as the doors were closing, drawing the ire of those standing in the corridor. He turned to see the three men glaring at him through the windows as the train departed.

The train was headed to Zurich, but he got out before it reached that station and took a taxi to the Langstrasse quarter to buy used clothing. After making his purchases, he rented a car and checked into a boutique hotel. He dared not return to his apartment—they might know where he lived. The package was due to be delivered the next day in Geneva.

Over dinner, he reviewed his situation. The thugs at the airport knew what he looked like and knew where the drop box was. But they didn't know about the man who had handed him the envelope. Rolf feared there must be a mole in his agency, so phoned Thomas to inform him.

Early the next morning, Rolf drove to the airport and parked. He transformed himself into an old lady and hoped that his "friends" at the airport didn't know which locker held the goods.

As Rolf approached the panel of cabinets, he noticed three different men who looked suspicious but were standing substantially away from the lockers. He walked slowly, back bent over, using an ornamental cane to steady his steps. In his other hand, he held a large carpetbag. As he neared the specific locker, the hairs on the back of his wigged head bristled as he felt the men's eyes burning into his stooped shoulders. Would they nab him after he opened the locker? The cane would come in handy if they did, but he was no match for three burly men.

Rolf opened the locker, took out the package, placed it in his bag, and turned to walk away. Out of the corner of his eye, he saw the men examining him intently; two had lowered their newspapers to their waists, and the third was taking photos. To keep up his cover, Rolf walked slowly, one step at a time: cane first, step, back leg forward, cane again. It seemed an excruciating long time, but none of them moved and when he peeked back, they were pretending to read again.

Back in his car, Rolf got out of the dress and donned an old man's outfit, a pair of baggy trousers, a yellowed shirt, a weathered sports coat, and a battered fedora. He removed the box from the bag and put it into a suitcase and set off for Geneva, a three-hour drive.

Now all he had to do was drop off the parcel. But since they knew his mission, they might also have more goons waiting for him at von Rothenburg's high security office. And, sure enough, when he arrived, he spotted three more men lounging awkwardly in the square in front of the building. How many men did his opponent have dedicated to this operation? He took the cane in case there was trouble.

As he slowly advanced on the building, limping this time as a caution against being recognized, he saw the men scrutinizing him. When he was in the middle of the plaza, still five hundred feet from the entrance, he heard a man shout, "Wait, I recognize that cane from the photos!"

Rolf broke into a run, his luggage trailing behind him. One man was moving to block his way to the door, so he swung his cane and whacked the man's knee, and he crumpled in front of him. Rolf jumped over him, bouncing the suitcase off his head, and kept running to the door, now with the case in his hand, to move quicker. But another ruffian was bearing down on him, getting closer and closer. Rolf half-turned and flicked the cane into his ankle, sending the ruffian down hard. Out of nowhere, the third thug appeared in front of Rolf, blocking his way to the entry, but Rolf landed a karate chop to his throat and proceeded into the security vestibule where he was greeted by armed guards.

Rolf collected himself, dusted off his jacket, put the suitcase on the roller belt, showed his papers to the senior officer, and stepped through the metal detector. A dapper young man appeared out of nowhere, reviewed his papers, and led him to von Rothenburg's office.

"We've been expecting you," Wolfgang said. "Any problems? I see you're wearing a disguise."

"Nothing I couldn't handle," Rolf said, and he took the box out of the suitcase. "I hope you don't mind if I change while you authenticate the artwork."

"Not at all. You can do that in the room to your left."

When Rolf returned, he observed Wolfgang carefully inspecting a large pedestaled red egg with a clock in its center.

"It's the Fabergé egg known as the Imperial Clock," Wolfgang said.

"What's it worth?"

"Oh, twenty-five million, give or take a few."

"That makes sense," Rolf said as he accepted his receipt for the egg.

Rolf walked into the square. The sun was shining and the water spraying from the fountain in Lake Geneva was creating a rainbow. He couldn't see any of the hoodlums that had tried to attack him. The police were questioning bystanders, but they ignored him; he now looked nothing like the old man who had entered the building. He spotted a

German restaurant, unusual for Geneva, entered, and seated himself at the bar. After ordering a draft beer, which came in a stein with a cap that you needed to lift to take a sip, he took a long swig to celebrate the success of his assignment.

THE PIER

It would be easy to get over the rail in front of him. Jack was standing at the end of the Anchorage pier, looking at the swirling mass of gray, freezing water. The lights from the harbor and the city behind him twinkled in the darkness. The air was heavy with salt and dampness. Jack listened to the waves slap the columns underneath him.

If he jumped in, he might make it to shore without succumbing to hypothermia. He'd need to swim out as far as he could stand it—then he wouldn't make it back. Of course, if he just stood here, the wind might freeze him before he made it into the water. It was February and a raging twenty degrees Fahrenheit. The water would feel warm and inviting. Jack continued to stare at the white-capped waves, translucent in the moonlight.

"What are you doing here?" a young woman asked after walking up to Jack's side.

"None of your business." Jack replied. "What are *you* doing here? This is my pier, and I'd like to be left alone."

"You don't own this pier!"

"Maybe not, but I was here first."

"Good. You go first, and then I'll be alone."

"You're here to jump, also?" Jack asked, puzzled. His heavy eyebrows and short-cropped beard were as black as the night and about as inviting. His square face and short, chunky stature formed a full-body scowl.

"Why else be at the end of nowhere on a night like this?"

"You go first!"

"No, you first!"

"Alright, just give me a minute," Jack said, his teeth chattering. "Damn it's cold."

"Yes. That's the idea, Hamlet."

"My name's Jack, not Hamlet!"

"Well, stop hesitating like Hamlet. *Jack*."

"OK, *Ophelia*. Drive me nuts and I'll do it."

Jack looked at the water, then he raised his head to gaze at the moon. A full minute passed, but it felt like an eternity in the chill of the night.

"Well?" "Ophelia" asked.

"I'll come back tomorrow. I never wanted an audience."

"Wait. Don't go! We'll jump together."

"No! I'm going to get a coffee."

"Can I come with you?"

"I thought you wanted to jump."

"I changed my mind."

"Suit yourself," Jack said over his shoulder. He was already three strides away.

Ophelia ran to catch up with Jack. Reaching him, she tucked her arm into his.

"What's this?" Jack said, looking with alarm at her gloved hand curled into his inner-elbow.

"I'm cold."

"That's the idea."

"It was the idea until you came up with coffee. Coffee is a warm idea, so I'd like to warm up."

"Whatever," Jack said, peeved. "What's your name, anyway? I can't call you Ophelia."

Ophelia looked at Jack and knitted her eyebrows.

"Well?"

"It's Jill," Jill said, making every effort to have the wind blow her name away.

"*Jill!* You're kidding me!" Jack said.

"No. That's my name: Jill."

"Where's your bucket? And the hill?"

"You're supposed to have the bucket and know where the hill is."

"Argh," was all Jack could utter in response.

They found an all-night diner. Its fluorescent lights beckoned, then blinded them. As they entered, the door tinkled, startling the waitress from her dozing. There was one other customer at the counter, nursing a coffee for dear life. He looked like he'd been there all evening and wouldn't budge until morning. They chose a booth by the window.

"Today's special is bacon and eggs with toast," the server said as she set down their menus. "It's a buck off regular price."

"I'll take a coffee and the special," Jack said, suddenly hungry.

"Just coffee, thanks."

The waitress gathered up the menus, brought them their coffees with a pitcher of milk, and went into the kitchen to prepare the meal.

"So, what are you in for?" Jack asked.

"In for? Oh, yeah. I got pregnant and my boyfriend left me. Then I had a miscarriage," Jill said, taking a tissue from her purse to dab the tears that had welled in her eyes. A letter with a patch of gold leaf glued to it fell out of her purse.

"What's that?" Jack asked as Jill shoved the envelope back into her purse.

"It's a letter to Emma. My friend Alisa suggested I write it to reach her. She said the gold leaf would ensure it reaches her." Jill's tone of voice told Jack that Emma was her lost daughter.

"I'm sorry for your loss. That must have been devastating after your partner split." Jack reached his hand toward Jill's, but then he pulled it back. His fingers were so numb, he couldn't imagine it would provide any comfort.

"I'm so depressed I don't know if I can keep living... You? Why were you out tonight?"

"I drank too much and passed out one night. My girlfriend didn't like it and she left me."

"So, we have a couple of things in common—lost partners and thoughts of suicide."

"Things in common?" Jack said, shaking his head in exasperation. "Well, maybe..." Jack looked at Jill. Her windblown hair still had curls where it met her shoulders, framing her face. She was dead white from the cold, but her brown eyes sparkled with a distant fire.

The waitress brought Jack's breakfast plate and two forks and knives. Jack put the plate in the middle of the table and pushed some cutlery to Jill. They ate in silence for a while. Their thoughts racing to the end of the pier and back.

When the bill came, Jack paid it and tipped the server generously.

"So, this was a date?" Jill asked, her voice lilting to form the question.

"No, it's not a date!" Jack said. But then he looked into Jill's eyes, which were welling up again, and said, "OK. Sure, if you like."

Jill's eyes twinkled as she looked at Jack through her lashes, her head bent.

"Our first." Jack said with the faintest trace of a smile.

ACKNOWLEDGMENTS

I would like to thank Tembisa Aborn and Julie Conover, two emerging writers whose work I'm sure you will hear much about in the future. They provided invaluable comments on early drafts of many of the short stories included in this book. I'd also like to thank Carlo DeCarlo for his diligent copy editing. Any remaining errors in facts, editing, and proofreading remain the author's sole responsibility.

ABOUT THE AUTHOR

K. E. KARL is the author of *Our Man in Mbabane*, a novel based on his experiences supporting the African National Congress in the 1970s and early '80s. His fiction has appeared in the *Pennsylvania Literary Journal, Lowestoft Chronicle,* the *Evening Street Review,* and *Gumshoe Review.* He has lived and worked in Oregon, London, Mbabane, Philadelphia, Maputo, Bangkok, New York, and Zurich. See https://kekarl. com/ for more information. Karl lives in Philadelphia.

www.ingramcontent.com/pod-product-compliance
Lightning Source LLC
Chambersburg PA
CBHW032119170626
46808CB00006B/2019